Esmahan Aykol was born in 1970 in Edirne, Turkey. She lives in Istanbul and Berlin. During her law studies she was a journalist for a number of Turkish publications and radio stations. After a stint as a bartender she turned to fiction writing. She has written three Kati Hirschel mystery novels. *Hotel Bosphorus* is the first and has been published in eight languages. It is also the first to have been made available in English.

D0723991

HOTEL BOSPHORUS

Esmahan Aykol

Translated by Ruth Whitehouse

BITTER LEMON PRESS
LONDON

BITTER LEMON PRESS
First published in the United Kingdom in 2011 by
Bitter Lemon Press, 37 Arundel Gardens, London W11 2LW

www.bitterlemonpress.com
First published in Turkish as *Kitapçi Dükkâni*
by Everest Yayinlari, Istanbul, 2001

Bitter Lemon Press gratefully acknowledges the financial
assistance of the Arts Council of England and of the TEDA Project
of the Ministry of Culture and Tourism of the Republic of Turkey

A CIP record for this book is available from the British Library
ISBN 978–1–904738–68–8
Typeset by Alma Books Limited
Printed and bound by Cox & Wyman Ltd, Reading, Berkshire

Hotel Bosphorus

1

I keep driving around, but there's nowhere to park near the shop. This thirty-minute search for a parking space every morning drives me crazy. It's intolerable. If I threw a wobbly here, what would happen? Would that shopkeeper on the corner come out to help me? Would the *çaycı* drop his tea tray and come running? And if they did, what then? I have to get a grip on myself.

Just as I'm calming down, some moron opens his car door in front of me. Thank you God. They say, things have to get worse before they get better.

The trouble is, Juan Antonio, my dear sweet Fofo, has been madly in love for two weeks and he's been acting like a real idiot. They supposedly met when Fofo spent a weekend in Şile on the Black Sea coast. Actually, it's quite difficult to believe they hadn't met before that, and if it wasn't Istanbul where they met, it almost certainly wasn't Şile. Anyway, they met and they fell in love. Alfonso teaches at the Spanish Cultural Centre. And Fofo? Fofo is meant to be helping me at the shop. Don't get me wrong, he really did help until two weeks ago. But now he's on another planet. We see each other at home of course, but only when he comes back for a change of clothes. Over the last two weeks, we've exchanged twenty words, if that.

I've been opening up the shop myself each day since Fofo turned into a lovesick butterfly. That means getting up early every morning and collapsing exhausted on the bed every night. In short, I no longer have a social life, and I never see my friends. I haven't even been able to talk to Lale properly.

Still, I love my work. But I preferred it when I wasn't tied to the shop ten hours a day.

"What could be more natural than for someone who loves reading thrillers to enjoy selling them?" Fofo would say. Actually, I thought the same thing when I first opened the shop. We often think alike.

Because of my beloved shop, I know all the crime-fiction readers living in Istanbul, or at least those who frequent Kuledibi. When I opened the shop three years ago, one of my first customers was Mick Jagger. I couldn't believe my eyes. Naturally, I didn't actually ask for an autograph or anything. But I found it very hard to resist asking for a photo of us together. I didn't even let on that I recognized him. Lale teased me a lot, saying my German inhibitions had got the better of me. I don't think it was anything to do with being German, I was just being stupid. I was afraid my credibility as a serious woman might be damaged if I let it be known that I recognized Mick Jagger... When I first opened the shop, I thought I was some sort of superwoman like Güler Sabancı. But that feeling didn't last long. If you slave away for ten hours a day, you soon feel like any other ordinary shop girl.

Still, compared with how things used to be, I'm OK. I've learnt to do the job well and I no longer have financial worries. I think I'll tell Fofo that if his stupid lovesickness continues and he doesn't come back, I'll find someone to replace him. Our Fofo has a mind like a middle-class housewife. I say this to his face. You know, the type who drops everything the moment she finds a man to support her... And then wonders what on earth she is going to do when she suddenly finds herself divorced.

This isn't the first time it's happened to Fofo. When we first met, a couple of years ago, he'd fallen in love with a Turk in Granada and followed him to Istanbul. He just dropped everything, packed a rucksack and jumped on a plane. His lover, Ali, was a lawyer, a lawyer who wore a cravat. It makes me shudder just thinking about him. How long could a person like that sustain a relationship with the Fofo we know? They were together for about a year, which I still say wasn't bad. Ali didn't tell his friends that he and Fofo were lovers. He didn't even introduce Fofo to them. For some reason, Fofo desperately wanted to meet Ali's cravat-wearing friends. He started turning up unexpectedly at the man's office, not because he thought Ali was cheating on him, but just because he hoped to meet his friends. Lale and I were at our wits' end. The last days of that relationship were particularly disastrous. Fofo spent his entire time sitting at home watching Turkish TV, which actually wasn't a bad thing because he learnt some Turkish and can now speak in TV Turkish. He comes out with inane phrases like, "Hi guys, I'm good to go", or "You take care now". But so what, at least he can be understood by anyone who watches television.

After we recovered from the Ali disaster, our lives took on some sort of order. Fofo moved into my house and started working at the shop. Dear Fofo, he's like a small child in an adult's world. I wonder what will happen to him with this new man. It's really been bugging me for the last two weeks.

I haven't met his lover yet. I've interrogated Fofo during our brief meetings, but he's a young lad in love and I can't trust a thing he says.

Lale tries not to show it, but she's worried too. She says to me, "You've become a real Turk, you're acting just like any Turkish mother with a son." I don't think she knows what she's talking about. She seems to think she's different. In fact, we're both worried because we know Fofo so well, and we know how he gets carried away. But quite apart from those worries, my nerves are frayed at the moment anyway and I find it intolerable when I can't find a parking space.

What's meant to happen is that you open up the shop, give it an airing, have a couple of coffees and then start the day, yes? But no, not today. The moment the key is in the door, the telephone starts ringing. I hate rushing, but I have to rush to open the door and then fly over to the telephone. A bubbly woman's voice is speaking in German. So early. It's really too much. A cheerful woman at this time of day is not on.

"I got your phone number from your mother. And I found your mother's number in the Berlin phone book..." she says.

"Fine," I say. "But who are you?"

But of course! It's Petra. A friend from my university days. We haven't seen each other for ages, at least fifteen or sixteen years. Actually, I'd kept track of Petra through the press and media because she is also my most famous friend. She's a star of the German cinema. It may not be world cinema, but have the Germans ever produced a world-class film star apart from Marlene Dietrich? And Marlene was more American than German.

Anyway, what was I saying?

Petra was in the drama department at college. After graduation, I packed my bags and set off for new horizons and we lost touch. Nothing unusual about that.

Petra had started to appear on television before I left Berlin. She even had a part in an episode of *Tatort*, which is still the best programme on German television. We didn't see each other for ten years or so while I was in Germany, but I didn't miss a single one of her films. I even went to see a German film at the Istanbul Film Festival just because she was in it.

I followed her films and read every word of her magazine interviews. But you know how it is if you have well-known friends: you develop feelings of inferiority and start thinking, "If we met in the street, she wouldn't know me," or, "If I phoned, her secretary would never put me through." I often felt that way about Petra. There was actually no reason for me to have these feelings, because we never met in the street and I never phoned her. I had no idea whether her fame had gone to her head. But now, I had Petra on the line, just as if we were in a novel. Clearly, since she was calling me, either she had not become big-headed, or she was no longer famous. Perhaps she had lost her celebrity status and become one of those unfortunates who live on the famous German state handouts. Maybe she'd been put through the all too common process of getting shoved around and spat out by Social Services before being handed the state pittance. Maybe she was seeking a way out of this social security nightmare and calling to ask me for a loan or a job. I had a bit of money, so I could give her a loan. In that respect, my friends generally find me more amenable than the German government. If she wanted a job, I could speak to Fofo straight away. Whatever the situation, she had picked the right person.

"I lost track of you," she was saying. "I tried so hard to get hold of you. Whenever I see someone from the old days, I always ask about you. I bumped into Alex at a film gala yesterday. He's living in Berlin and working as a cameraman. He said he saw you a few years ago in Berlin and that you were staying at your mother's place then. That's when I thought of calling your mother. How stupid of me not to think of that before. Anyway, why didn't you ever call me?" I was lost for words, dumbfounded. I couldn't say, "I didn't call you because you're famous." In any case, we weren't really the kind of buddies who were going to keep track of each other, but that's another matter.

"Are you coming to Germany?" she asked.

At that moment, I had no intention of going there, but I said, "I don't know." That's because I just might have gone, if it was to see Petra. I liked the fact that she didn't seem too aloof, even though she was still famous. It would be worth going to Germany just to see her again.

I put the telephone down and stared at it for at least ten minutes. It lay there like a black-tailed snake on the table, but I wasn't marvelling at its wonders. I was just dumbstruck. Petra was coming. She was to play the starring role in a joint Turkish-German film to be set in Istanbul, and would be staying for over a month. She didn't want a loan or a job. She didn't even want to stay at my place during filming, but just wanted to see me again to chat like two old friends. She would give me tips on the best face cream for getting rid of bags under the eyes, or maybe teach me her special trick for getting limescale off the kitchen sink without damaging the enamel. She just wanted to do what two ordinary women might do, and behave as if she wasn't famous.

I collected myself and decided to start the day by making coffee, even if it was late. There's a corner of the shop that we use as a kitchen, where Fofo and I make gallons of tea and coffee. If we used Recai, the local *çaycı*, all the time, we'd spend a fortune. By the time we'd made our kitchen habitable, he'd have earned enough from us to replace his shack with a skyscraper, which would inevitably be razed to the ground in the first 5.8 Richter-scale earthquake.

Actually, I adore *çaycıs*. You simply can't compare them to those soulless vending machines... A *çaycı* will always know your name, and if you take sugar in your coffee. He knows when you want tea and when you want coffee. If your *çaycı* is anything like our Recai, he knows if you've left your lover, if you've made up, how late you stay out at night or if you spend an evening in front of the television. In short, he knows more than he should, but you have nothing to fear from a *çaycı* unless you're mixed up in illegal activities. Everybody knows everything about you anyway; the gossip network in Istanbul is so strong that one more makes no difference at all.

Of course, it isn't easy to keep up to date with every item of gossip in a city as huge as Istanbul. That's why Turks are forever talking on their mobiles, whether it's in the street, when they're out for dinner with their sweethearts, or even in theatres and cinemas. I think

Alexander Graham Bell must have had Turkish genes. If not, how come Turks are so infatuated with this contraption?

Once again, I arrived home in the evening feeling completely wrung out. I hate days like that. Dealing with customers, the constant ringing of the telephone, people coming, people going… It was bedlam. I'd barely had the strength to turn the key when it came to locking up the shop. I also paid the price for having gone to work by car. In Istanbul a car is nothing but trouble; it doesn't make life easier at all. It's an ancient city where the roads are very narrow, especially where my shop is in Kuledibi, an area that dates back to Genoese times.

Sometimes I think that everyone must spend their whole time out in the streets and that none of the city's ten million or so people ever goes home, day or night. The streets are constantly teeming with people and cars. Ten million people – it's easy to say, but it's the size of a nation.

In the end, parking difficulties and traffic congestion in Istanbul play havoc with your nerves. But I'm lazy. It takes thirty minutes to get from home to the shop, on foot or by car. I go by car.

Work was so busy that day that I didn't have time to revel in the fact that Petra had called. But the moment I got home, I went straight to the telephone like any normal Istanbul citizen, or *İstanbullu* as we say, and called Lale. She knew about Petra; we had been to the film festival together to see her film and I'd offered to translate some of Petra's magazine interviews, but Lale wasn't interested. She can be irritating like that. Still, what can I do? She's my best friend.

After Lale, I wanted to phone Fofo, but I couldn't because I didn't know his number. I sat and smoked three cigarettes in fifteen minutes, then called Lale again. Her phone was engaged. I went for a shower to pass the time and tried again. Still engaged. I considered jumping into the car and going to her house, but couldn't be bothered. I pressed the redial button; it was still busy. As consolation, I called my ex, whom I keep dangling and mostly ignore. You might as well know that. Yes, that telephone was engaged too. I cried myself to sleep from nervous exhaustion. I dreamed I was trying to crush Alexander Graham Bell's head with the telephone handset, and Madame Curie was shouting, "Murder! Murder!" I woke up in a sweat.

The next day was Saturday, the best day of the week, followed by the second best day, Sunday. Many serious-minded or acquisitive citizens sit at their desks on the first of these happy days. I am definitely not in either of those categories. On Saturdays, the closed sign hangs firmly on the door of the shop, unless Fofo is depressed and decides to do some cleaning.

On Saturdays, I join my neighbour and dear friend Yılmaz at the local café, where we lie in wait to pounce on passers-by. Yılmaz is in his fifties; he's a short, fat, bald man who works in advertising. A real stereotype. He knows everyone; he tells me all the gossip and then tells everyone all about me… However, I decided long ago that I didn't care, and I count Yılmaz as one of my buddies.

So, on Saturday mornings, Yılmaz and I buy our pastries from the bakery, our newspapers from the corner shop, and settle ourselves in the café. This happens at about ten o'clock. All Cihangir society walks past us. Some we entice to our table, while those who know better merely wave and walk on. When we tire of gossiping, Yılmaz and I go to the cinema together if there is a good film, or if not we go home...

We have a mutual understanding that Yılmaz buys the newspapers and I buy the goodies from the bakery. Actually, I don't read newspapers during the week, so this is something different for me on Saturdays. And change is good, isn't it?

It's become a habit. Yılmaz always arrives before me, exactly on time. He never passes up an opportunity to berate me for my lack of punctuality, especially as I'm German. I retaliate by saying that Turks always assume Germans are punctual, hard-working cold fish, and then insult Yılmaz by saying he's no exception. As you might guess, the worst insult for Yılmaz is to be told that he's just like everybody else.

I can't let this pass without mentioning some strange prejudices that Turks have about Germans. For instance, Turks are amazed to see a smiling, cheerful German. They love it when I laugh, because they think I've become really integrated into the community. I haven't yet convinced anyone that I used to laugh when I lived in Germany, even if only occasionally, and that it didn't mean I was excommunicated from society. I even know people who think the reason I came to live in Istanbul was that I couldn't remain in Germany because I was too cheerful.

The fact that my name is Kati seems to suggest to Turks that I'm a different kind of German. You might not believe this, but I've actually met Turks who think there are only two German names: Hans for males, and Helga for females. Why? I have no idea.

I had been in the café for fifteen minutes and Yılmaz still hadn't made any jibes about punctuality and being German. He was probably too preoccupied with his work. The advertising company where Yılmaz worked was in the midst of a financial crisis, like many companies in Turkey. People were apparently going to be laid off. I suggested that if this happened to him, he could take the job that Fofo was probably going to give up. He looked at me as if I was joking. So what? Was I supposed to feel bad if I couldn't pay him a monthly salary of ten thousand dollars?

Petra had said she would call me again when her dates were confirmed, that is to say when the Turkish Cultural Ministry and the producers had completed their paperwork. Two weeks passed while I waited for Petra to let me know when she was coming. Naturally, I wasn't idle during that time. I found Fofo and told him in no uncertain terms that I would replace him if he didn't come back to the shop. I had no intention of working myself into the ground. Actually, there aren't that many people who want to work in a crime-fiction bookshop, but I expected to find someone eventually.

Fofo dithered and couldn't give me a straight answer. He was starting to get on my nerves so I interrupted, "In that case, I'll take on a temp for three months. You can use that time to decide what you want to do. Are you going to spend your whole life going after some boy or other, or are you going to learn to stand on your own two feet?!"

After this meaningful and important speech, I slammed the door and left. I don't think Fofo had ever heard anyone talk to him like that, or had a door slammed in his face. He was infatuated with Alfonso. However, I also had pride that had to be salvaged.

A few days later, I went to see my friend Candan, who has a large bookshop in Beyoğlu. I wanted to find someone who would be right for my shop. Candan was great at that sort of thing. Whenever I put a request to her, she would provide exactly what I was looking for. And it happened again. She called up four or five places on her mobile and, one hour later, a pleasant-looking girl was sitting opposite me: Pelin.

Pelin was a student at Istanbul University, studying English language and literature. She was from İzmir and had come to Istanbul to attend university and get away from her family. For seven years, she had been both studying and working, which was why she had been at college for so long.

"I've no problem with that," I said. In fact, this was a point in her favour. "I hate people who work too hard," I added.

"Even though you're German?" asked Pelin.

We worked out a division of labour. It wasn't fair, but it was a division of labour of sorts. Pelin would open up the shop three days a week, thus allowing me to sleep until noon on those days. Having worked in a bookshop before, she quickly adapted to the job. Her comings and goings were observed reproachfully by *çaycı* Recai, who couldn't bear the fact that he knew nothing about her.

Fofo is my friend, so I don't like saying this, but Pelin worked at least five times harder than Fofo. When it was her turn to open up the shop, it happened exactly on time. She would dust the books, tidy up, put flowers on the table, and there would always be fresh tea and coffee, providing she wasn't feeling depressed. She came right up to my German standards... Her only fault was that she didn't like thrillers. But I thought we'd overcome that in time. It didn't really bother me.

Pelin said she liked books and working in a bookshop, even if she didn't like thrillers, but she often hinted that she wanted more pay. Turks from good families don't talk openly about their financial aspirations, they just drop hints.

"Let's see, who knows what might happen?" I said, adopting her hinting technique.

I was thinking that, if Fofo didn't return within three months, I would sell my car so that I could employ Pelin. However, my dear friend Lale saved me from that financial problem. The moment she met Pelin, she started to tell her all about me and how, despite spending my first seven and last thirteen years in Istanbul, which is twenty years and almost half my life, I had still not shed the damaging effects of my awful German peasant background. She said I was a typically stingy German. I never turned on a light at home unless it was necessary; I didn't even fit halogen bulbs because of the expense, and only shame prevented me from spending my evenings in candlelight like other Germans. Once Lale started, she didn't know when to stop; she went on and on, saying that to save money I refused to take taxis, served used teabags to my guests, tried to get people to pay for their own meals in restaurants, and so forth. I can't let that one pass without comment. Whenever people pay separately, Turks call it "doing it the German way". They give me sidelong glances, then look at each other and snigger as if I single-handedly created the "German" way of paying bills.

Anyway, Lale spilled everything about me. I kept quiet because I didn't want to have to defend those intolerable Germans. And of course, it went in my favour, as you might expect. Pelin now thinks I am an oppressed migrant and feels more sympathy for me. I feel confident that if someone offered her three times her current salary, she wouldn't want to leave me.

2

It was May when Petra called for the second time.

The magical Istanbul spring was about to turn abruptly into summer. I would have liked Petra to see Istanbul in spring: to drink tea under the shade of ancient pine trees in the gardens of magnificent Ottoman palaces, to walk along mimosa-scented streets, to shiver in the dampness of the Byzantine underground reservoirs, to light a candle in one of the churches as the muezzin chants the call to prayer, to stretch out in the warm spring sunshine on grass damp with early morning dew looking at the Hippodrome and the Sultan Ahmet fountain, to eat artichokes prepared in olive oil at Hacı Halil Restaurant…

"They've only just got the filming permit," Petra was saying. Turkish bureaucracy, like German bureaucracy, is famous for its cumbersome paperwork, so I wasn't at all surprised by this delay. The filming had been planned to start at the end of April, but now could not start until the beginning of June.

"You've missed the spring," I said to myself.

I told her that I would meet her at the airport. Her hotel was near my house so there would be no problem about seeing each other.

*

I spent one of the longest hours of my life in a smoke-filled café at Atatürk Airport, which had recently been expanded in an attempt to compete with Athens. Anyone who thinks the number of cigarettes people smoke increases with the excitement of seeing off or greeting loved ones should know that Turks never need an excuse to smoke. It was therefore quite normal to sit in a café where clouds of smoke burned my eyes and made it almost impossible to breathe.

I had no option but to join the overwhelming majority of smokers.

Was I excited that I was soon to see Petra? Had I missed her? I tried to visualize her face and the effects the years would have had on her. What a life she had led – and what had I done? I had just stopped myself from going deeper into a misplaced, mistimed evaluation of my life when the airport Tannoy system announced that Petra's plane had landed.

Going to meet Petra at the airport was a complete waste of time. The place was full of journalists trying to get a glimpse of the film crew arriving in Istanbul. But it was soon over. A team of minders moved into place to get Petra away from the crowd. However, she noticed me waving and jumping about trying to catch her attention, and yelled at the men to let me through. A few seconds later, we found ourselves next to each other, surrounded by a wall of beefy men who were steering us towards the exit.

I hadn't taken account of the fact that my long-time friend was a star of sorts and the crew clearly hadn't expected that Petra might have a half-witted friend like me in Istanbul, because they had a limousine waiting for them. When I saw the limo, there was no way I was going to say, "Don't go with these brutes, I'll go and get my car." My '82 Peugeot would have cut a pathetic figure next to that awesome limo. In the end, I yelled out, as she was being bundled into the car, that I'd see her at the hotel. Petra waved at me to signal OK, the chauffeur put his foot down and they sped off.

I drove along the coastal road from the airport to the hotel, with the Bosphorus opening out into the Marmara Sea on one side and a mixture of lower- and middle-class neighbourhoods with their tall ugly buildings on the other. The traffic wasn't too bad for a Friday and I was even able to drive at full throttle. It was perhaps the first time since coming to Istanbul that its frenzied beauty, which had survived both indifference and efforts to destroy it, did not play on my mind. I was thinking of Petra. For a moment, that expression on Petra's face... As if her heart needed recharging, as if she couldn't cope with life, as if she was broken in some way... There is a kind of sadness that can permeate people's faces and expressions that is not visible in photographs... No cream or cosmetic surgery can eliminate it... It is a deep, dark, incurable sadness.

Eventually I got stuck in traffic at Sarayburnu, by which time the sun was setting over the Golden Horn. I needed to phone Pelin to tell her not to wait for me, but to close up the shop and go home. I had left saying I wouldn't be long, but that was hours ago. I hadn't taken account of the Friday-evening traffic and I was battling against the sort of traffic chaos that a true *İstanbullu* would avoid at all costs. If I went to the shop, I would be late for Petra at the hotel; if I didn't go to the shop, Pelin would be left waiting there for me.

It was a moment when a mobile was essential, utterly indispensable. I could have parked the car and looked for a phone booth, but even if I'd found a parking space, it was unlikely that there'd have been a phone nearby. I was about to explode with frustration when I had an ingenious idea. The driver in the car next to me looked like a good local family man, so I called out to him.

"Excuse me, do you have a mobile by any chance?"

The poor man was surprised by my question, of course. These days, even primary-school kids have mobiles, so why was I asking?

"I need to make a really urgent call. I didn't reckon on the traffic being this bad. May I use your mobile?"

After I'd finished, I didn't know how to turn it off, so I gave it back to him still on and offered to pay for the call. "No need, ma'am," said the driver.

To demonstrate his contempt for me, he bit his lower lip, leaned his head to one side and raised his hand, saying:

"Don't mention it."

I arrived at Petra's hotel in a real state. My poor mangled body was sweating profusely, my legs were stiff from constantly pressing the accelerator, brake and clutch, and my face was a grimy yellow from all the cigarettes I had smoked to fend off exasperation. I was much later than my worst estimate. They must have arrived long before me. It was ridiculous to think of that enormous limo negotiating the traffic, don't you agree?

When I asked the lad on reception to call Petra's room to tell her that I'd arrived, I couldn't understand why he was looking at me with such respect and wonder, until I realized he thought I was one of those "rich celebrities". In spite of the state I was in!

Petra was staying in a suite with a magnificent view; it was almost larger than my apartment. This time, we had a proper reunion scene. There was nothing exaggerated about it. Any two Germans who had not seen each other for years would have had this sort of reunion. Imagine you are in a Schlöndorff film: Schlöndorff is the best at German reunions. For instance, there was just such a scene in *The Legend of Rita*, which I saw on my last trip to Berlin: two female Red Army militants go on trial together, and then go to Palestine where they kidnap a man from prison and kill a policeman... You'd think that facing such dangers would make even these soulless individuals close, wouldn't you? But no, not them. Anyway, years later these two women meet by chance in East Germany. There they have a proper reunion, a real German reunion, exactly like the reunion between Petra and me: handshakes, and a reluctant brush of the cheeks. That's all. No embraces, no hugging, not even any mutual stroking of backs... As you see, despite my aversion to clichés about nationalities, I sometimes have to concede that certain German stereotypes do in fact reflect the truth.

But let's get back to what I was saying. Petra apologized profusely, saying that she hadn't realized her arrival would create such a stir and wished she'd told me not to come to the airport.

We were both too exhausted to wander round the streets, so Petra suggested ordering food from room service and abandoning any idea of going out. I must admit I felt grateful to her for this.

It had been so many years, yet during our first ninety minutes together we spoke little about our past lives.

However, I couldn't rid myself of the dark thoughts that had been with me since I first saw her at the airport. Petra had become much more reserved. We hadn't been very close before, but I had never felt she was quite so distant. Usually when I meet up with friends after a long gap, we comment on how much has happened since we last met and how we won't lose touch again. But this was totally different. I couldn't say why, but the tension I sensed was not merely because we hadn't seen each other for years. Something was missing. It wasn't to do with me, and it wasn't our relationship. Petra had lost something. Was she seeking what she had lost in me?

I left her draped over the sofa, weak with exhaustion. Several thoughts were swirling round in my head. "Like a cooking pot", as Turks say. My head had become exactly like a cooking pot. I collected my car from the hotel car park. The Friday-evening rush had even reached Ortaköy, but I set out into the traffic once more, towards the bridge that would take me across to the Asiatic side of the city. I was going to see Lale. I didn't want to spend this Friday evening sitting at home all alone.

When I opened my eyes the next morning on the sofa bed in Lale's study, the first thing I did was to phone Yılmaz. I told him I couldn't make our customary Saturday-morning rendezvous. Next I phoned Petra... She said she'd woken up ages ago and had even had breakfast; she was about to find out what the day's programme was, and would call me straight back.

We were drinking coffee over the empty breakfast dishes in the garden at Kuzguncuk when the telephone rang. It was Petra. She was calling to say that we couldn't meet until dinner that evening. They were very much behind schedule and the director wanted to start work right away without losing any more time.

I felt pretty fed up, but I didn't let Petra know that. Anyway, it wasn't her fault. It was nobody's fault, but what was I supposed to do on this lovely Saturday?

Lale was in an even more depressed state than I was. And it was the only day she didn't go to work. We spent half an hour wondering what to do and finally decided to spend the day at the beauty salon. At least after a day investing in your beauty, you come out looking reasonable, especially if you're a middle-aged woman on the lookout for a cute guy.

I got back home in the early evening feeling tired but relaxed, and I looked wonderful. One of the things I like best about Istanbul is this grooming business. Here it's a part of everyday life; people go to hairdressers and beauty salons as a matter of course. In Germany, most people, or rather all but my mother and her friends, trim and colour their own hair. And as for manicures, pedicures and skin treatments, well they're out of the question. That's why the streets are full of people you'd really rather not set eyes on. Munich is different. There you find people with some sense of beauty, but the hordes of sluts in Berlin discourage you from going outside. The specimens you encounter on the metro and in the streets disgust me.

Actually, the most stylish people in Berlin are Turks, but only second- or third-generation Turkish girls in headscarves. These headscarved girls are unbelievably stylish. Of course, when I say stylish, they're not wearing the latest Jil Sander creation. They create their own fashion and stick to it: fashionable platform shoes, black nylon trousers that look cheap but have a modern cut, artificial leather coats... Headscarves in the latest colour, long jackets that tone with the colours in the headscarf...

The first generation of headscarves in Berlin was completely different, however. I think headscarved people understand this difference between the two generations better than anyone. When I was a child, we used to say "penguins" for the first generation of headscarves. They were all from the same mould, but a tasteless mould. In their grey smocked coats, those short fat women waddled from side to side just like penguins. They were a world apart from the young girls of today, even though they all wear headscarves.

It was eight o'clock by the time I found out that the evening meal Petra had promised me was not going to happen. Apparently it was essential for her to be with the film crew that evening. We chatted a bit on the phone. She was fed up. It was quite clear she would much prefer to be with me. I was really sad, and in fact felt quite anxious for her. I wanted to tell her that she was looking tired and listless, but I held my tongue. It's better not to tell people things like that. If they take you too seriously, it can be harmful.

You can imagine what a crisis it was for me when my Saturday-evening plans collapsed. Everything seemed even more desperate than it had in the morning. I certainly had no wish to sit at home with my manicured nails, blow-dried hair and nourished skin. Nothing could persuade Lale to set foot outside on her single day off, so I didn't even try calling her. I found Arzu on her mobile. Arzu always had something going on, and that evening was no exception. She said she was meeting friends, some of whom I knew, at ten o'clock in the Cactus. They were going to decide what to do for the rest of the evening when they got there. We said we'd meet in a few hours' time and rang off.

The Cactus Café is an important place in Istanbul. I think its main feature is that all its customers know each other. The regulars are all the same type: journalists, writers, advertising people... A small group of yuppies had recently started to tag along, but I think they must have been given the brush-off, because I haven't seen them recently.

I was about to leave the apartment and was just making a final check of my hair and make-up in the full-length mirror in the entrance hall when the telephone rang. It was Petra. She had managed to get rid of the crew that evening; we could meet if I still wanted to. I just couldn't tell her that I'd made other plans in the meantime.

"I'll pick you up in half an hour," I said.

It was no problem getting Arzu on her mobile again to tell her I wouldn't be coming. Arzu wasn't bothered about such things.

This time, I was sensible and left the car at home. If you can just grit your teeth and tolerate the drivers, it's cheaper to take a taxi than to pay car-park fees. And you don't have to deprive yourself of a drink. The traffic police are more tolerant towards women drivers but, even so, they have started imposing alcohol limits on Istanbul's nightlife.

It took me less than half an hour to reach the hotel. I called Petra on the internal phone at reception. As I sat in the lobby waiting for her to come down, I thought about where I could take her for a late evening meal. Should we go to a good Turkish bar, or one of the posh or halfway-posh fish restaurants on the Bosphorus? I couldn't decide.

When Petra emerged from the lift fifteen minutes later, it was obvious that we couldn't set foot inside any reasonable restaurant, let alone a posh or halfway-posh place. She had suddenly turned into a middle-class German tourist, wearing exercise sandals with white sports socks, baggy shorts and a T-shirt that, by Istanbul standards, could have been a duster. Asked which of us the film star was, any three-year-old would have pointed at me. So that was why the name Petra Vogel hadn't had the same effect at the hotel reception desk as the previous day. I wondered what she had been doing during the half-hour or so I spent on the journey and in the fifteen minutes I was waiting in the lobby. Once again, I kept quiet because I am not as rude as most Germans, especially Berliners.

I needed to think fast and make a quick decision. So, I had a long-standing friend wearing white socks and exercise sandals, yes. I'd met her after many years and there was still some kind of bond between us, yes. But did I want to announce to the whole of Istanbul on this beautiful night that I had a friend like this? No. I dashed over to Petra, and pushed her back into the lift.

"I don't feel very well. It's so crowded outside... Istanbul traffic, Friday night..." I stopped to catch my breath. "What about sitting out on your balcony and ordering something from room service as we did the other evening?"

"Are you sure you don't want to go out?" asked Petra, looking me up and down in disbelief.

"Definitely," I said.

The cost per night of Petra's suite was probably equal to six months' rent for my place, but the hotel was worth every penny. Can a hotel room make a person happy? Well, this one could. I dragged Petra inside, shut the door and was engulfed by a wave of indescribable happiness.

We called room service, ordered some wine and cheese, and settled ourselves on the balcony where we could hear soul music coming from the hotel's famous jazz bar. I had no complaints about my life, and Petra was in good spirits. I became talkative and told her about my past love affairs and what I had been doing with my life.

I talked first. Then it was her turn.

By the time I'd reached a state where I could no longer listen to what Petra was telling me, it was long after dawn. I'd consumed far too much alcohol in an attempt to fortify myself against the misery my friend had suffered. We left the hotel and walked in silence as far as Dolmabahçe. The early-morning coolness made me feel better, even if it didn't quite bring me back to reality. We went to the stand-up café next to Dolmabahçe Palace where, along with other drunks, we drank tarry tea to obliterate the feeling of helplessness and those turbid nightmares of the past...

It was almost noon when I returned home. I had a long shower and went to bed, where I tossed and turned at length before going to sleep. The moment I was alone, Petra's words overwhelmed me all over again. What she had gone through was very real and very scary. Something seemed to have changed in me, as if an innocent part of me had been corrupted. And this corruption seemed to have been chiselled into my heart. I was still a small child when I first learned how other people's personal tragedies could affect you and destroy your belief in human nature. Even if you had not yet had any personal experience that might be termed true tragedy... Still...

My sleep was interrupted by the phone that kept ringing and the nightmares that kept appearing. When I finally decided to get up, I felt more tired than ever. As Petra's words went round and round in my head, everything started to seem even worse than the previous night. I didn't think I could spend an evening and night alone at home, so I jumped into the car to see Lale, which is what I did whenever something painful happened to me.

When I opened my eyes the next morning, Lale had long since left for her beloved work. However, it was still so early that normal people, even civil servants, had not so much as thrown back their duvets. I called Pelin at home, waking her to say I wouldn't be at the shop until the afternoon. I wanted to collect my thoughts and decided I'd feel better if I strolled around the streets for a bit or went to a comedy film. In the end, I could do neither. I had to see Petra. It would help just to sit at the edge of the film set. The only way I could escape this distress, this nightmare, was to be with Petra and see how she dealt with it. That was the best solution I could think of.

My heart seemed to have been replaced by an enormous hole that was draining away my feelings. I wanted to cry, but couldn't. I wanted to talk to Lale, yet the previous night I'd been unable to say anything. I'd spent the whole evening staring vacantly at the TV. Thanks to the sleeping pills Lale recommended, I'd managed to sleep a couple of hours, but no more. Now, at the crack of dawn, I was sitting in the garden with a coffee cup in my hand wondering how I'd get through the endless hours ahead of me.

At about eight o'clock, I decided to give Petra a call. I thought she must be awake because they were filming that day. In any case, Petra was not the type to sleep until noon. For many people, discipline and success go hand in hand, whereas people like me flounder around in the muddy waters of life without managing either.

The phone in Petra's room was answered by a male voice speaking in Turkish. At eight o'clock in the morning, a Turkish-speaking man was answering the phone in Petra's room. "God, what hypocrites people are!" I thought to myself. Only last night she had been saying that she couldn't embark on any new relationship after her experiences, and that she was now crippled in this respect. Yet, only three days after arriving in Istanbul, a Turkish man, no doubt dark and handsome, was picking up her phone. My first reaction was to put the phone down on this fellow, and to erase Petra and everything she had told me from my life. But I was rather old for such behaviour.

"May I speak to Petra, please?" I said.

"Madam, are you calling from Istanbul?" he said, in a thick Black Sea accent.

I managed to stop myself saying, "What's it to you?" I thought this might seem rude to a Turkish man.

"Why are you asking?"

"I'm Alaatin, a police official from Ortaköy Police Station. We're here to investigate a murder. If..."

Murder... Murder...

I had only ever encountered that word in novels; it was the first time I'd heard it uttered in real life.

"Mur… mur… murder?? Who? Is it Petra?" I said with difficulty. Alaatin hesitated uncomfortably; they weren't supposed to give out information, and he didn't have the authority to do so anyway.

"Look, Inspector, I'm Petra Vogel's friend. What I want to know isn't a state secret, I just want to know if Petra is OK."

Addressing Alaatin as "Inspector" was a good idea, I can tell you. He immediately dropped his guard.

"Miss Vogel is fine, madam."

"Thank you, Inspector," I said, this time as a reward.

Petra was OK. Or rather, Petra was not the person who had been killed. Yet since the murder investigation was taking place in Petra's suite, the murder had some connection with Petra. That probably meant that someone in the film crew had been murdered. What else could it be? I decided to get dressed and go to the hotel straight away for the following reasons:

One, Petra might need me. These policemen had to be addressed as Inspector, the inspectors as Chief Inspector, and the chief inspectors as District Chief of Police. I was one of the few people who realized that bestowing such imaginary ranks opened many doors in the police force. The time had come for me to use this knowledge.

Two, a murder had taken place. I'd been reading crime fiction since my childhood, and selling it for the last three years. I was no longer just an ordinary reader. The time had come for me to offer my theoretical knowledge for the benefit of society.

I left the apartment and jumped into my car. For two months now, things had kept happening. First, my dear friend Fofo had found a lover and disappeared from my life without a second thought: I was missing Fofo. Then, I'd received what would normally be considered excellent news: my most famous friend, Petra, whom I hadn't seen for years, was coming to Istanbul. As soon as we'd had a chance to talk properly, she had related a story of tragic proportions that would darken the world of the most hard-hearted person. And now her suite was full of policemen from Ortaköy Police Station.

I tried to keep calm by repeating to myself that Petra's situation was far worse than mine, and that these mounting problems now made former disasters in my life, which at the time had each seemed so important, seem like sweet memories. That was the positive side of it all. I didn't even want to think about what might lie in store for me in the days ahead.

While trying to cross the Bosphorus Bridge in Istanbul's morning traffic to reach the European side of the city, I thought about what had happened to Petra during the years we were out of touch.

3

When we finished university in the early eighties, I decided to loaf around and travel the world for a while. I was going to live like a belated flower child. Petra, however, was progressing rapidly in her career. I hadn't even left Berlin when Petra Vogel's name started to be heard in the world of cinema and television. It wasn't exactly fame at this stage, even in Germany, although we all realized she had the potential for fame. It was around then that we lost contact. Even though we didn't meet up, we continued to get news of each other through mutual friends. The last I heard from these friends was that she was living with Wolfram von Haagen, one of the leaders of the socialist student movement. Wolfram was a brilliant medical student, an effective orator and a very handsome man. Half the girls I knew were in love with him. When I heard that Petra was with him, I couldn't believe it. Petra was my friend, yes, but I couldn't really understand what someone like Wolfram saw in Petra. It wasn't because I was jealous, that's just how it was.

Petra and Wolfram were complete opposites. Deep down, Petra wanted to be a housewife. She had an appetite for life, but only seemed to be working at her career until she found a man to rescue her and take her away from ordinary life. She didn't have a real passion for her work. I still think of Petra in that way. She is very competent, but in my view the reason she remained a B-grade actor was this lack of passion.

As for Wolfram, I listened to a few of his open-house forums at university. Unlike Petra, he could become passionate about anything. He spoke about revolution and socialism in a way that could persuade the most ardent rightist and excite the most soulless person.

I heard that they were living together shortly before I set off from Berlin with my rucksack for new horizons. At that time, according to Petra, her relationship with Wolfram was already deteriorating day by day. Wolfram had fallen out with his rich aristocratic family, who in turn had cut off their rebellious left-wing son. The task of making ends meet fell to Petra. Wolfram couldn't decide what to do with his medical degree and spent all his time running around between protest meetings and political gatherings.

Petra began to yearn for a child. Marriage was unfashionable in the mid-eighties, and the only way of making a relationship official was to have a child. In those days, a child really did make a relationship permanent. However, Wolfram always insisted that he didn't want a child and that there were numerous other things he wanted to do in life. He clearly began to fear Petra's determination and, as a way out, started looking for work outside Germany…

Petra was two months pregnant when Wolfram joined a group of doctors researching malaria in various parts of Africa. Wolfram insisted on Petra having a termination, but she was stubborn and said she would raise the child on her own and wanted nothing from Wolfram. That was their last conversation. Three months later, Petra heard that Wolfram had left for Africa.

Petra was now five months pregnant and in a desperate dilemma. She had never really wanted the child for herself, only to save her relationship. But since Wolfram had no interest in children… Anyway, their relationship was now over, despite their unborn child… She had failed at that game… Petra had to think what she would do if she had this child. She went to several quacks asking for a termination, but no one would abort a five-month-old foetus. Petra finally accepted her fate: she would have the child and accept that Wolfram had left her.

Petra had no chance of finding work as an actor with her expanding belly. After giving careful thought as to how she was going to manage, she gathered her few belongings together and packed them off to her mother's house. Her mother lived alone in a remote house near a tiny village on the bank of the Rhine. Petra stayed with her there until she had recovered from the birth. They agreed that her mother would take on the role of looking after her grandchild and Petra would send money each month.

Hardly anyone knew that Petra now had a son. She had told friends and acquaintances that the pregnancy had been terminated, perhaps because her pride was not reconciled to Wolfram's departure. Her mother also concealed the fact that the child was Petra's. Even though in big cities it might be perceived as "modern" for a single woman like Petra to give birth to a fatherless child, in a German rural outpost on the Dutch border it would still have been considered a manifestation of immorality. Nobody discovered the truth. In the village, they knew young Peter as the son of Petra's married older sister who was living in Korea. They didn't even tell the child the truth. He knew Petra as his aunt.

Peter was a beautiful child. Beautiful and, like all children brought up by elderly people, rather sad. Petra would go to the village to see her son once or twice a year, and she even managed one holiday with him during his first six years of life.

As for Wolfram, he had settled in Africa where his name soon became well known in the field of malaria research. They had run into each other once in Berlin, but he hadn't even asked what happened about the child. "Maybe," Petra said, "someone told him that I'd had a termination. Still, I did expect him to ask. When he didn't, I kept quiet about it."

Petra was rapidly climbing the ladder of fame; she had no time for anybody, let alone her son. Over time she saw less and less of him, but they would talk on the phone. Her mother kept saying that the child was very withdrawn, that he had no friends at school and that the reclusive life he lived was not suitable for a child. Petra would forget her mother's anxieties the moment she put the phone down, but she would always send extra money the following month.

Work prevented Petra from seeing her son on his first day at school and on his sixth birthday. A few days after this birthday, Petra's mother called to say that Peter had not returned from school that afternoon. Petra dropped everything and went to the village.

Peter was a lonely child. He had no friends. He was the worst student in the class and was always causing problems. On that day, some children had seen him talking to a man when they came out of school. Peter was looking unusually happy. He was laughing out loud, holding the man's hand and turning round to look at the other children. The man was tall, blond and wearing a suit. The children couldn't give any more details about the man's appearance. According to the village bar owner, a man of this description had been seen several times in recent weeks. However, no one had spoken to him and he had done nothing to attract attention. He was an unremarkable outsider in a tiny village.

Peter's grandmother said he'd come home with a huge teddy bear on his birthday, but didn't say who had given it to him. "But," said the old woman, "somehow he changed after that birthday. He started doing his homework as soon as he came home, tidying up his room and he looked happier than ever before."

His teachers had also noticed the change in Peter. "He's shown more interest in everything over the last two weeks. It's given us all hope," they said.

Peter did not have even one friend, not a single person with whom he could share a secret. The children at his school did not know why Peter talked to that man, why he looked happy, why he held his hand or when he first met him. Peter did not keep a diary of what had been happening; in fact he couldn't really write properly. But he did draw pictures. A child psychiatrist working with the police tried to discover clues in his pictures, but came up with nothing.

Peter's photograph was distributed to all the surrounding towns and villages, but nobody had seen the boy since he was abducted. His pictures were shown on news bulletins and crime programmes in a bid for information from anyone who had seen him or knew his whereabouts. There were over three thousand telephone tip-offs, but the outcome was zero. Petra hired a private detective, who was unable to find even the smallest clue.

Two months after his abduction, Peter's bruised and mangled body was found in Belgium, in woods surrounding a village near Brussels. The tiny body had been violated. The perpetrators were never found and there were no clues.

4

The driveway to the plushest and costliest hotel on the Bosphorus was seething with police and journalists' cars. The murder of one of their clients was probably not good for the hotel's reputation, at least in the short term. However, I doubt if the owners, whoever they were, cared very much.

The hotel was swarming with men who were obviously plain-clothes policemen. I had become really curious about the identity of the victim. When I asked at the reception desk where Petra might be, a woman told me Miss Vogel wasn't speaking to journalists.

"Oh, for God's sake," I murmured to myself.

"I'm her friend. Please, would you call her, wherever she is, and tell her that her friend Kati is in the lobby?"

Without even waiting for me to finish my sentence, the woman turned her back and was gone. I noticed a male receptionist who looked a bit more human; this time I said I was Petra Vogel's friend and wanted to see her. Clearly everyone had got out of bed on the wrong side that day because he also stood his ground, saying, "Miss Vogel doesn't want to be disturbed, madam."

When I asked him to at least give her a message, it did no good at all.

I am not a person to give up easily, so I decided to go and eat something in the hotel café and work out a strategy. The journalists were also there, picnicking in the café and, like me, waiting for the right moment to pounce.

I approached a woman sitting at a table apart from the others. I recognized her vivacious appearance and dyed blonde hair from one of the commercial news channels. Using all my networking skills, I told the woman that I recognized her from television and enjoyed her work, and I asked if she would answer a question for me.

She didn't look very impressed by my flattery. Nevertheless, she said, "Of course, sit down."

"I'm Petra Vogel's friend and I want to see her but they've changed her room, and reception won't give me her new room number. Perhaps you…"

The woman glanced quickly at her notebook as I was talking, and murmured, "Petra Vogel, Petra Vogel."

"I haven't written down her room number. Wait here, I'll find out from my colleagues and let you know," she said, and disappeared.

I didn't understand who she meant by "colleagues", but I didn't think the woman would come back anyway. She probably thought this was outside her remit. After all, she wasn't there to perform a public service and satisfy someone just because they flattered her. So I was amazed when, two minutes later, she returned with a list in her hand.

"You're looking for the film star who was staying in the Topkapı suite, aren't you?" she said.

"Yes," I replied eagerly.

"They've moved her to Room 724."

I looked gratefully at the woman.

"May I ask you another question?"

She nodded her head.

"Who was the murder victim?"

"Don't you know?"

She looked at me vacantly as if she couldn't understand why she had gone to so much trouble for me.

"It was the director of the film your friend was starring in," she said.

The director of Petra's film!

What was his name? What was it?

There was no point straining my memory. I had never known the man's name, so how could I remember it?

In fact, I must have seen his face when I went to the airport to meet Petra. But in that crush I hadn't had the slightest idea who was the film director or who was the gaffer. I didn't think I'd read anything about this director anywhere. What had Petra said about him? Then suddenly, I realized that Petra and I hadn't discussed the film at all. I didn't even know what part Petra was playing, never mind the director's name or the subject of the film. This blonde journalist undoubtedly knew much more about these things than me.

I called Room 724 from the telephone at reception. It rang for a long time, but nobody answered. That initiative had also failed. I could have gone home or to the shop, but curiosity got the better of me. I returned to the café and sat at a table where I could overhear what the journalists were saying. I waited and waited, jumping up every so often to dial 724 on the internal telephone. What I was waiting for, I had no idea, but I certainly knew I wasn't just waiting in case I was needed by Petra.

Realizing I wasn't going to get the information I wanted by eavesdropping on the journalists at the next table, I interrupted their conversation with an apology and asked the name of the murder victim. The plumpest and friendliest-looking of them asked, "Why do you want to know?"

"I just wondered if he was someone famous," I said. "The hotel is swarming with police and journalists."

"He wasn't actually famous or anything," said the friendly young man. "His name was Kurt Müller, but I've never heard of him."

I was getting into conversation with yet another man who probably didn't even know who Steven Spielberg was.

"Hmmm," I said to myself. "Kurt Müller," I repeated. What an ordinary name, even for a murder victim.

The chubby young man looked eager to talk; he pulled his chair up to my table and pointed towards the packet of cigarettes lying on the table. I held out the packet to him. "Who's this Kurt Müller?" I asked.

"A film crew came here from Germany three days ago to shoot a film. You must have read about it in the papers," he said, lighting a cigarette. "The murdered man was the film director. He was found dead in his room at about five o'clock this morning… How he died, we don't know either. The police haven't made a statement about anything yet. All we know is that there is a murder suspect."

It was long past noon and I decided I couldn't spend the whole day sitting in that hotel café. I could go to the shop and relieve Pelin, which would at least be doing something useful. I used the internal telephone at reception to try Petra's number one last time. I no longer expected an answer, and there was none.

Any reader who thinks I was feeling mad with frustration is utterly wrong. On the contrary, I was absolutely calm and simply following my destiny. Could life be any more straightforward than this? I, a seller of crime fiction, had glimpsed an opportunity of being an amateur detective, but now that opportunity had disappeared, and I would just carry on with my ordinary life. The shocks of the last few days, and the effect of all the coffee I'd drunk while waiting for a murderer to approach my table with his murder weapon and bloodied hands, was more than enough for me. I decided it was time to give up my passion for detective work.

However, for some reason, this opportunity for detective work, which I thought had been and gone, was not going to leave me alone.

You now know all about Istanbul traffic and the problems of parking. It's really not a pretty sight to see me struggling with all that. However, I managed to reach the shop without leaning out of the window to swear at the driver in front of me or quarrelling with pedestrians at red lights. I tell you, I was totally at peace and content with my lot.

When I entered the shop with two toasted cheese sandwiches in my hand, I had a pleasant surprise. Petra was sitting in my rocking chair. The moment she saw me, she jumped up. "Where have you been?" she cried out almost hysterically.

I didn't say, "And where have you been?" She might have been waiting there for a long time. To be honest, I was surprised that I hadn't thought of calling the shop.

"What's going on?" I said, biting into my toasted sandwich.

Petra had gone out to eat with the film crew the previous night. She hadn't stayed out long before returning to her room to go to bed. Later, she learned that the others didn't stay up late either; they'd split up at about twelve thirty. The plan for the following day had been to do some filming outdoors, so they needed to get up early in order to meet in the lobby at four thirty. The whole crew turned up at the appointed time except for the film director. They waited awhile, assuming he hadn't managed to wake up. Five minutes later, they called his room. When there was no answer, they waited some more. They couldn't do any filming without the director, so there was nothing else to do but wait. At about five fifteen, after many telephone calls, one of them suggested going up to his room, saying, "He put away a lot of drink last night. If he's unconscious, he won't hear the telephone." Everyone thought this was a sensible idea. It was no secret that the man drank like a fish. At reception they were told that a hotel room could not be opened if the client was inside. They then consulted the hotel night manager, who in the end agreed that the wardrobe mistress, who was the director's closest friend, could go up to the room with a member of the hotel staff.

The wardrobe mistress had barely left before she returned looking flushed, shouting, "They've murdered Kurt!"

Petra didn't know how he was killed; she hadn't asked. The fact that she wasn't even curious made me uneasy to be honest, and my mind started working. Bearing in mind that even the wardrobe mistress had said, "They've murdered him," and she had only been in the room long enough for a glimpse, it must definitely be murder. Based on my experience from novels, I was in a position to say categorically that if a murder was as obvious as this, it was carried out with a gun. Yet even if it was a gun, you'd think an ordinary wardrobe mistress might think it was suicide before jumping to the conclusion that it was murder. Why didn't she say "He's committed suicide", or "He's dead"? I had more than one answer to that question:

1. The wardrobe mistress killed the director.

2. The murderer had just not bothered to dress it up as suicide.

3. The wardrobe mistress was a reader of thrillers and so didn't believe people could die a natural death or commit suicide.

4. The director was killed by a gun, but the location of the bullet wound meant it was impossible for him to have fired the shot himself, and the wardrobe mistress had realized that with a single glance, which meant the wardrobe mistress must have more expertise than that of a mere reader of crime fiction. I had no idea whether retired doctors and homicide detectives found employment as wardrobe mistresses these days.

5. No murder weapon was visible and the retired homicide detective-cum-wardrobe mistress noticed that at a single glance.

After reviewing all these possibilities, I came to the conclusion that my thought processes were getting me nowhere.

To be honest, I don't like the police. Some might claim that it goes beyond mere dislike, but let's not get into psychoanalysis. Suffice it to say, I will go out of my way to avoid a cop. My mother has always impressed on me, ever since I was little, that I shouldn't make friends with the police, and I've never forgotten that. Actually, I should point out that our views on the police are the only ones we have in common. As far as my mother and I are concerned, policemen are creatures who transcend nationality. For us there's no difference between British, Turkish, Mexican and German; as policemen, they're all as bad as each other.

However, the god in the police uniform who had stepped through the shop door thirty seconds ago was a potential threat to this one view I shared with my mother, that ultimate tie that bound us together. I tried to hide the fact that I was completely bowled over by him and, pretending not to see the police car in front of the shop and Recai standing outside the shop window, I said, "Yes, constable. Is there a problem?" I addressed him in that way just to upset his ego, because I could tell he was at least an inspector.

"I'm from homicide, ma'am. Inspector Batuhan Önal. I'd like to ask you a few questions if you have time," he said.

Now, any readers who know anything about Turkey and Turks will realize that was a strange statement for an inspector to make. For the others, I think a short explanation is required. For instance, the name "Batuhan" is not the sort of name for an inspector to have. Usually, inspectors have ordinary Turkish names such as Ahmet, Ali, Mehmet or even Orhan. Batuhan is the sort of name given to pop singers. Any family that names its son Batuhan has definitely not brought him into the world to be an inspector.

It's quite possible that Inspector Batuhan Önal's mother took up gambling and his father became a heroin addict, after that dreadful day when their son stepped into the Police Academy. He had undoubtedly been the cause of a family tragedy, yet this brute of a man was standing opposite me smiling, as polite as you please, as if he'd had nothing to do with what befell his family.

In my view, it was not only strange but unnecessary for an inspector to be as polite as that. That morning at Ortaköy Police Station, when I had spoken to a policeman, whose name I'd forgotten but was undoubtedly ordinary, he had addressed me as "madam", from which I inferred the following: the European Union should stand firm because Turkey has set its sights on becoming a member and is taking decisive steps in that direction. That was why the Turkish police were showing respect for human rights.

"Did you mean me?" I said. I jerked my head towards Petra and added, "You're probably looking for my friend Petra."

Petra was still sitting in my rocking chair, rocking away as if she hadn't a care in the world.

The mixture of surprise and delight on Inspector Önal's face suggested that he hadn't noticed Petra until I mentioned her. However, he tried not to show it.

He glanced at the notebook that he took from his pocket, "Your friend Petra... Yes, I'm looking for Petra Vogel," he said. This time, I pointed towards Petra. Recai was still standing outside the shop window following what was going on. To make him go away, I ordered three teas.

Inspector Önal knew English, of course. I would have eaten my hat if I'd heard any other policeman utter a single word in any foreign language, but I was not at all surprised that he knew English. Who would have expected anything less from him?

Petra's English always used to be bad, and it still was. In fact, Petra had no talent for languages. Even her German was bad. Because Petra and Inspector Önal had no common language, I was going to have to do more than merely listen to their conversation.

Petra repeated almost word for word what she had told me ten minutes before, no more and no less. Inspector Önal didn't say a word until she finished speaking; he just made a few notes.

"Would you please ask her whether she heard anything unusual when she returned to her room last night?" he asked when Petra had finished. He was asking me, but his eyes were fixed on Petra.

I couldn't contain myself, slave to my curiosity that I am.

"What sort of sound do you mean? The sound of a gun?" I blurted out.

"The sound of a gun? Where did you get that from?" He turned to look at me.

"I don't know.... I mean... How was Müller killed?"

"Oh, that's what you mean. No, no, he wasn't killed with a gun." He laughed teasingly. When he laughed, his gleaming white teeth were visible. I tried, with difficulty, to concentrate on what he was saying rather than on the man himself.

"Actually, you might say it was rather original," he continued. "It happened when he was having a bath. While he was in the tub, a hair-dryer was thrown in, and it was switched on..." He stopped for a moment; this time he smiled ever so slightly and said, "A very frothy murder."

I repeated this to myself: a very frothy murder. Fine, but was that what made it original? The fact that it was frothy?

Inspector Önal looked straight at me impatiently, "Will you please ask Miss Vogel whether she heard anything unusual last night? Did she see anything? Any information that might seem insignificant to her could be useful to us. Please would you translate this?"

I translated what he had said.

"No," said Petra, with certainty. "I heard nothing and I saw nothing. I went to sleep as soon as my head touched the pillow. I was very tired."

He noted down what Petra said.

"We'll have to take another statement from Miss Vogel in the presence of an authorized interpreter." I think he thought that might have sounded rude because he hastily added, "I have to have an authorized interpreter for this to go on file."

He then turned to Petra and continued, "Miss Vogel, if you wouldn't mind coming to the police station tomorrow... Just ask for me when you arrive. Shall we say five o'clock?"

I translated what Inspector Önal had just said to Petra, hardly daring to think how I would react if a policeman asked me to come down to the station. However, Petra calmly continued rocking back and forth. With the same calmness, she confirmed that she would come to Inspector Önal's room at five o'clock the following day.

"Would you also ask whether Miss Vogel has any immediate plans to leave Istanbul? The other members of the film crew say they are going to stay and finish the film, but if Miss Vogel has different ideas I would like to know."

I translated this into German as well.

"No, I'm not going anywhere. We're going to finish the film, with or without Müller," insisted Petra.

After Inspector Önal had noted that down, he got up and shook her hand. Before extending his hand to me, he asked whether he could come to the shop again later.

"Why?" I gulped. "This has nothing to do with me. I simply know Petra, that's all."

"I didn't say I was coming to ask anything about the murder. I wanted to chat to you about crime fiction. I read a lot of thrillers too."

I have to admit that made me feel more at ease. I screwed my face up into an awkward smile and said, "Actually, I want to ask you something too. How did you find me?"

"Madam, that's our job. We believe we can learn something from anyone who might have some connection with a murder, however remote."

"Yes, but that doesn't answer my question," I said.

For a moment, he studied my face carefully.

"The film crew said that Miss Vogel had a friend who is a bookseller in Istanbul. It wasn't difficult to find your shop." He spoke as if mine was the only bookshop in Istanbul, but I didn't question him further. There was no point. I needed to save my energy for later.

Once Batuhan had gone, I suggested that Petra should stay at my place. She didn't want to. I didn't really insist. It was up to her.

She got into a taxi and returned to her hotel.

5

The next morning, I woke up at nine o'clock, which surprised even me. Excitement has a good effect on me. It was nearly ten o'clock and the temperature was soaring towards thirty degrees by the time I'd settled myself in the local corner café with the newspapers.

It was front-page news in all the Turkish press. I read every word, but there was nothing I hadn't heard from Petra or Inspector Önal the previous day. Only one of the newspapers gave any information about the film director: Kurt Müller was born in Bielefeld in 1952. He had made two films, *The Night After the Rain* and *In the Footsteps of Eternal Love*, neither of which had achieved any success. I'd never even heard of them.

All the newspapers agreed that this film, *A Thousand and One Nights in the Harem*, was likely to provoke comment. The film set was intended to conjure up the images in the best-selling book of that name by the famous Italian writer Giacomo Donetti. The managing director of Mumcular Films, which was co-producing with a German company, was Yusuf Selam. He had issued a written statement the previous day saying, "Our art and artists have been touched and tainted by this evil." If you ask me, his claim was a bit much, but never mind.

Yusuf Selam added that they would resume filming as soon as possible despite this tragedy, and do everything to ensure the film's success.

After reading all that, there was one point I couldn't erase from my mind: if it was based on a novel by Donetti, one of today's best-selling writers, why had it been handed over to a second-class director like Müller?

The temperature was now rising rapidly to forty degrees. The sun was burning down on my head as I flew along the steep streets of Çukurcuma towards my air-conditioned shop. Once there, I went straight onto the Internet, the greatest human invention since the wheel.

News about the murder appeared in most of the German newspapers under the same headlines: Murder on the Bosphorus. Any documentary or novel about Istanbul inevitably squeezes in the word "Bosphorus" somewhere or other.

The news items in *Westdeutsche Zeitung* and *Tagesblatt des Ostens* were a bit better than the others, but there was still no proper information about Kurt Müller in either of those papers.

Who was this Kurt Müller? I tried putting his name into my favourite search engine, which produced a total of 1,634 Internet sites. A wave of despair swept over me. However, given that one in four Germans is called Kurt or has the surname Müller, that number was not at all surprising.

I opened up a hundred or so of the 1,634 websites, until I got bored. Only a handful of them contained anything to do with the Kurt Müller I was looking for, and those only showed recent press items about the film and murder.

I was about to thump my computer when I remembered my friend Sandra, a retired doctor living in Bielefeld. If Sandra didn't know this man, she would undoubtedly know someone who did. I got on the phone immediately.

I had just eaten an early supper of Trabzon pitta bread and was washing it down with gallons of green tea, when I caught Inspector Önal gazing through the shop window. Pelin had left work early and gone to the cinema.

This time, Batuhan Önal was in plain clothes. But don't assume that wearing plain clothes meant he was well dressed. His grey flannel trousers and short-sleeved white shirt were a poor substitute for his uniform. However, to be honest, he would have looked good in a sack.

I beckoned him inside. He didn't wait for me to do it again. As soon as he entered, I said, "Would you like some green tea? It's fresh."

"Don't trouble yourself," he said, which in Turkish means "That would be very nice."

"Has there been any progress with the investigation?" I asked as I went to the kitchen to fetch a cup.

"Very little. We haven't been able to speak to all the members of the film crew yet. Taking statements through an interpreter is a slow process. Actually, I doubt if the statements will produce anything more of interest. Everyone says roughly the same thing."

"OK, but what do you know about the victim?" I called out from the kitchen.

"Victim? You know..." He stopped. I was standing with a cup in my hand in front of the striped curtain separating the kitchen from the shop.

"Who'd want to kill the poor man? And why? I understood him to be a quiet, harmless type," I said.

"Would you call him harmless? I don't know. You're right that in his capacity as a film director he was harmless. He didn't amount to much as a film-maker and it's unlikely that that was his main job." There was a silence. My heart jumped as I took in what he was saying. Had I got it right – that Müller's murder was linked to his lifestyle and relationships?

"Of course, these… These are not things you should talk about in public," he said. I didn't understand what he meant just at that moment, but I would soon find out.

"It's a complicated case, as far as I can see," I said, all the while wondering how I was going to get him to say more.

"Yes, it's pretty complicated."

"Was the film director mixed up with drugs?" I said out of the blue. This possibility, which had just occurred to me, almost flew from my lips of its own accord. I'm not usually so indiscreet.

Batuhan looked startled: "Where did you get that idea from?"

"It's one of the first things people think of."

He looked at me admiringly and then, thinking he'd changed the subject rather skilfully, started telling me about how much crime fiction he'd read. Actually his knowledge of detective stories wasn't bad at all, and he loved reading Raymond Chandler. After about half an hour of him rattling on like that, I managed to escape to the kitchen, saying, "I'll make some more tea."

He looked at his watch and, without lifting his head, said, "It's a bit late for tea." When he raised his head, he didn't look at me. He spoke in a voice that was almost inaudible.

"What if I asked you out for dinner? We could talk more comfortably," he said.

I replied in German, "*Sie sind schneller als die Polizei erlaubt.*"

Very politely, he said, "Excuse me, I don't know German."

I'm not so polite. I translated it into Turkish as "You're a fast worker."

In fact, the Trabzon pitta bread I'd consumed just before he arrived was lying undigested in my stomach like concrete, but there was no way I was going to refuse Batuhan's dinner invitation. I had to look after my own interests. Ever since the previous morning, I had been flapping about trying to find something about the murder but had so far made little progress. The only way was to get Batuhan talking. A good meal, some wine... I changed this to *rakı* when it occurred to me that this man, who grinned half bashfully, half shamelessly when glancing at the open neck of my blouse, was actually a policeman. A kebab with *rakı* would have Batuhan warbling like a nightingale.

Without appearing too eager, in fact as if I was doing him a favour, I accepted the dinner invitation. Immediately I added, "But, I'm going to choose where we go. OK?"

There's no harm in being open with you. I was afraid he would either suggest going to one of the wine bars in Beyoğlu where my friends go, or to some haunt whose only customers were his police colleagues. Normally, I leave the business of choosing a place to the man; if it turns out to be awful, I'm as good as the next woman at expressing my views through facial expressions and gestures.

I did a quick mental scan of all the possible places we could go to and finally settled on a kebab restaurant in Yeşilköy.

Although Yeşilköy is on the European side of Istanbul, it is quite a long way from the triangle of Beyoğlu, Cihangir and Kuledibi where I lived and worked; in fact it's a long way from anywhere. To give readers who don't know Istanbul an idea of the distance, Atatürk Airport, where I went to meet Petra the other day, is in Yeşilköy.

Yeşilköy is also on the coast of the Marmara Sea and is one of the outlying districts of Istanbul where you see some greenery, and houses with gardens. Of course, for that reason, house prices there used to be at a premium. I say "used to be" because that was the case until the Marmara earthquake. Although it hasn't been proved that the ground in that district has little resistance to earthquakes, anyone in a position to move away from Yeşilköy and the surrounding area has done so. Now, Yeşilköy consists of kebab restaurants trying to evoke memories of better days, and widows and pensioners who don't have enough money to move out.

We left the shop and Batuhan ran ahead to open the door of his red Renault. I thought this choice of car was rather colourful for a policeman, or at any rate for a murder detective.

We hardly spoke as we drove along the road from Kuledibi to Yeşilköy. I took advantage of not being the driver to think about the last four days. It was only four days since I had driven along this road – with completely different thoughts in my head.

The Saçıkara kebab restaurant in Yeşilköy was still standing, and it was open, thank God. I hadn't visited it for years, and now I couldn't even remember why I had gone there then.

The inside was like a vast hangar. Under the fluorescent ceiling lights, even rosy-cheeked Turks looked like pasty Scandinavians. For some reason I can't fathom, Turks really love fluorescent lighting. I've never liked its glaring brightness, or the restaurant's overweight middle-class regulars. The ventilation unit was working full pelt to cool all those strange people who eat kebabs in the heat of summer, myself included. At that moment, I didn't like the place at all, or perhaps I should just say I wasn't crazy about it.

I practically ran to the most distant table.

We ordered a couple of meze dishes, a kebab with aubergine, and *rakı*. I don't care much for kebabs made from fatty meat and, to be honest, I don't really like *rakı* either; the mere smell of it is enough to turn my stomach. For that reason, I spent the whole evening raising my glass and just pretending to drink.

Thinking that our conversation was not going to venture beyond types of kebab, detective stories, problems of the police profession, or Turkish politics, I raised my *rakı* glass once again and, feeling nausea in my throat, asked hoarsely, "Who do you think could have murdered Müller?" Just like that, out of the blue. "Earlier today at the shop, you said you suspected that Müller's main job was not that of film director, but…" All of a sudden, I couldn't decide how to finish the sentence. I didn't want to scare off Batuhan, yet I didn't know how to put the question indirectly. Perhaps my Turkish was not as good as I thought. Or? Or it was simply a personal characteristic of mine? All my life, I've been a direct person. I wasn't going to change suddenly just because I wanted Batuhan to talk. In any case, this game of talking round the issue was beginning to get tiresome.

"Inspector," I said. I slid my backside around on the chair, turned to the left and put my right elbow on the table with my hand under my chin. I thought I looked rather impressive, like a female columnist, as I gazed straight at the man sitting opposite me. "You're a fellow reader of crime fiction, so I think you'll understand me. Deep down, we all want to be a detective really..."

"Or a murderer," said Batuhan.

"I must say, I've never heard of a crime-fiction reader who turns into a murderer," I said. I smiled, adding, "Or am I on your list of suspects? Is it because I read detective stories?"

"Well you not only read them, you sell them too," he said, laughing at his own joke.

"Wonderful. A female seller of crime fiction commits a murder. But why?"

"Because the murder victim had deserted the bookseller's close friend and was about to sack her."

"What do you mean?" I said. I think we'd stopped playing games by then.

"According to what we've learnt, your friend Petra was in love with Müller. Just about everyone in the film crew knew that. Apparently, Müller and Petra had a row after they arrived in Istanbul and Müller decided to give the starring role to a Turkish actress called Ayla Özdal. In short, when Müller was killed, Petra was about to confront him on both these counts."

It was no longer possible for me to maintain my female columnist pose. I now understood what Batuhan had meant when earlier that evening he had said, "I don't think we'll learn anything more of interest from the statements of the film crew." They'd already obtained enough interesting material from those statements.

I reached out for a cigarette from the packet on the table and lit it with the lighter he held out for me. As I exhaled, I leaned my head slightly to the right, looked at him seriously and rather disdainfully, and said coldly:

"Do you think that is sufficient motive for a normal person to commit murder? I mean, the person we're talking about isn't a cold-blooded murderer; she's an ordinary person, like you or me. In fact she's someone with more to lose than either of us. She's a famous actress." The extent of Petra's fame was perhaps questionable, but that was not our priority just then.

"As far as I'm concerned, what I said constitutes a very possible motive for murder. For someone famous, it's not insignificant to lose both a lover and a job at the same time." He took a large gulp of his iced *rakı*. It wasn't a pretty sight.

"Anyway, I'm not saying that Miss Vogel committed the murder. We don't have sufficient evidence to prove that. As you know, everyone is innocent until proven guilty." He uttered this last sentence somewhat arrogantly and took a mouthful of *rakı*. If he went on like this, he would very soon be drunk.

"Let's suppose that Kurt Müller intended to sack your friend. Mind you, I'm not saying he was, we're merely discussing possibilities. There may be nothing in it, we're still investigating." He also lit a cigarette. "But if that is the case, Miss Vogel would have had more to gain financially if Müller had been killed after he broke the contract." He rubbed his fingers as if counting out banknotes.

If you ask me, Turks have started to take money matters more seriously since the latest economic crisis. He continued to bombard me with words without letting me get a word in edgeways.

"If Müller had been killed a few days later, the contract your friend signed would have been cancelled by the film company and, according to the conditions of the contract, Miss Vogel would have had full rights to compensation." He stopped for a moment and grinned at me.

"Whichever way you look at it, it doesn't look good for Miss Vogel," he said.

"And the police," I thought, "there's something vulgar about them, even when they're handsome."

"Is Petra the only person on your list of suspects?" I asked.

"No, no," he replied unconvincingly.

"So who else is there?"

He shrugged his shoulders and muttered something.

"For instance, could this be a crime of passion?" I asked.

"The underlying motive for the murder might be love, money or revenge. But what mainly interests us is who committed the crime, not the reasons why. We leave it to lawyers to prove motives and establish what bearing they have on the crime," he said. He looked at me as if to measure the effect of his grand words on me. His eyes had become bloodshot from the *rakı*. I realized then that I no longer found him attractive and that the situation had become serious. I was in a place that I only knew about from going to the airport, and I was eating kebab and drinking *rakı* with a policeman who thought my friend Petra was a murderer.

When I awoke the next morning, the air had not yet started to heat up. I phoned the corner shop to give them my order. The shop owner Hamdi had noticed that I'd been buying all the papers for the last two days. As he filled the basket I'd lowered from my window, he grinned up at me and asked, "What's up, Kati? Keeping track of world events then?"

Please! I really don't need such a display of intimacy first thing in the morning. But I must be getting used to these Turkish ways because I just laughed it off.

A two-day-old murder was obviously stale news as far as the newspapers were concerned, because a photograph of film star Ayla Özdal showing her bum while playing tennis appeared to be more appealing than a passport photo of Müller's pock-marked face.

All the papers I bought gave plenty of space to what Ayla Özdal had said the previous day at a press conference with her manager. She had said mournfully that her great talent was not appreciated in Turkey, and that while she had all the qualities necessary for representing Turkish cinema abroad, this chance had been snatched from her at the last minute because of a crazy murder. Her manager spoke a bit more sense. He said it was true that, following the murder of the director, the future of the film was uncertain, but Ayla was Turkish cinema's greatest asset and she would undoubtedly receive new offers and represent her country abroad excellently.

After giving details of Ayla Özdal's press conference, the newspapers ended with a few lines saying that Müller's murderer had not yet been caught, but that finding this person was definitely a top priority for the Istanbul police.

I immediately called Petra. I think I woke her up this time.

"The Turkish papers are full of news today that you were about to be sacked," I said, instead of saying good morning. I was cross with Petra because of the things I'd heard from dubious sources which made her the number-one suspect, but not so cross that I wasn't prepared to ask her to her face whether or not she was Müller's lover.

"About to be sacked? Where did that come from?" she said. I don't think she was fully awake yet.

"That's what the papers are saying," I said. For a moment we both remained silent, waiting for the other to speak. I didn't even consider telling Petra that I already knew this before reading about it in the papers. You only give as good as you get, or as the Turks say, I was prepared to "match her bread with an equal amount of *köfte*", but no more.

"Was I going to be sacked?" she said. It was clear from her sleepy voice that she didn't believe it.

"Yes, apparently you were going to be sacked," I said, thinking it would be better to speak to her when she wasn't so sleepy.

"If you like, we could meet in an hour's time in the hotel lobby, go for breakfast somewhere, and I'll translate what the Turkish papers are saying."

After that, I immediately phoned Lale.

Lale was publishing director at Turkey's biggest newspaper, *Günebakan*. She therefore had access, and could get me access, to information from police and reporters. She was also my closest friend, as you know.

65

She promised to arrange for me to meet two reporters who had been writing about the murder for *Günebakan* over the last two days. Her secretary would phone in ten minutes to give me a time and place.

While waiting for the secretary to phone, I passed the time in front of the wardrobe trying to decide what to wear. Actually, it was a complete waste of time. I could wear anything because as soon as I left the house, I would be bathed in sweat. In the end, I put on an open-necked white cotton T-shirt and mauve linen trousers, and sat down at the dressing table. As I applied blue shadow to my right eye, the phone rang. It was Lale's secretary. Two reporters would be waiting for me in the Kuledibi café at four o'clock. What a great person Lale was. Despite being so busy, she'd taken the trouble to consider where might be the best place for me to have a meeting. No one else in her position as publishing director of the enormous *Günebakan* would have bothered.

I hastily finished applying shadow to my other eye. This time I didn't dither over whether to take the car or not; I hailed the first passing taxi.

The number of people taking taxis had fallen owing to the economic crisis, and it seemed to me that taxi drivers had calmed down. Twice in the last four days, I'd managed to get out of a taxi without having a row. It was unbelievable.

I was early for my meeting with Petra, so I took a short stroll through the streets near the hotel. I came across a jazz bar where a cleaner was vacuuming the cigarette ash from the night before and collecting up bottles. Finding a place to sit, I put my chin in my hands and looked out towards the beautiful Bosphorus, a sight I never tired of. But this time I was just staring vacantly, thinking about what had been discussed the previous night. Batuhan suspected Petra of carrying out the murder. That was the situation, whether I liked it or not. However, his suspicion made no sense if, as he'd let slip in the shop, Müller was not really a film director.

I saw Petra waiting for me as I entered the hotel lobby through the main sliding doors.

We strolled along the tree-lined road, full of exhaust fumes, which led to the tea gardens in Ortaköy, chatting about German cinema, without any mention of the film or its director. With some *simits* from a street seller and mature *kaşar* cheese from a corner shop near the square in Ortaköy, we went to sit in the tea garden nearest to the sea. Ortaköy is an interesting district. The gulf between classes, which is glaringly obvious in Istanbul, is just as evident here but somehow doesn't oppress people. For instance, we were sitting in a fairly cheap municipal tea garden, yet just behind the garden we could see luxury chauffeured cars queuing up at the doors of the former Esma Sultan Palace for a society wedding. Ortaköy is one of several districts in Istanbul where the jet-set and ordinary people can live and enjoy themselves in close proximity.

As soon as the waiter left us alone, Petra started relating what she had done the day before. It was the first time since she arrived that she'd had an opportunity to look round Istanbul and, like all normal tourists, she had visited Sultan Ahmed. Until that city tour, my friend had probably thought the beauty of Istanbul consisted of the view of the Bosphorus she could see from her hotel window. She started to describe with surprised excitement the wonders of Topkapı Palace, Ayasofya, the Underground Reservoir and the Sultan Ahmed mosque, which she had visited during her tour of the historical peninsula the day before. But I interrupted her: I'd spent the last thirteen years, as well as my first seven, in Istanbul and had had frequent visitors who all told the same stories, with the same expression of enthusiasm and wonder. I found it nauseating. Also, I preferred to talk about the fight between Ayla Özdal and Petra over the starring role, and about the love affair between Müller and Petra.

"Did you know you were about to be sacked?" I asked as my first line of attack.

"No, I heard it for the first time this morning from you," she said. She rummaged around in her handbag for a packet of cigarettes. "What are the papers saying?"

I had to satisfy my own curiosity before answering Petra. After all, I'd had to put up with that endless chat about stupid German films all the way from the hotel.

"Do you know Ayla Özdal?" I asked. I pushed a newspaper with a photograph of the woman towards Petra. She pulled the paper towards her and studied the photograph.

"This woman? No, I don't know her." She rummaged in her bag again and produced a lighter.

"Are you sure?"

"Yes, I'm sure. Definitely," she said. "What are the papers saying?" she asked huskily as she lit her cigarette.

"The papers are saying that your former director Müller wanted to give your part to that woman. Or rather, that woman claimed at a press conference yesterday that Müller would have given it to her, if he hadn't died."

"Well, that's interesting. You must be wondering why she would say a thing like that."

"Yes," I said, "that's exactly what I'm wondering."

I was just pondering that Petra's interest had clearly been aroused by the Ayla Özdal incident, when she said, "Give me your mobile for a moment."

My friends think I've assimilated well in most respects, but I've never seen anyone fall in line with Turks like Petra, and she'd barely been in Turkey for a week.

"Is this the time to talk on the phone?" I said, rolling my eyes.

"Don't you want me to find out whether or not I was really going to be sacked? I'm going to ring the Turkish producer and ask him. If all the papers are writing that I'm to be sacked, they can say it to my face."

It was a rare moment when a mobile could have been of use and I was unable to enjoy it. Without even finishing our tea and *simits*, I dragged Petra towards the nearest telephone, which was at the hotel because of course we couldn't call from a public booth in Ortaköy.

I decided to put off telling Petra that I knew about her relationship with Müller until later. Whatever happened, that was to be my main striking blow.

It was not at all easy to reach the Turkish producer. First, Petra spoke to the person who answered the office number she had been given. She had no need of any help from me because it was obviously someone who spoke German. This person said they couldn't give out the producer's mobile number, because he was on holiday and didn't want to speak to anyone. Looking annoyed, Petra put the phone down and dialled the number of the film company in Germany. It took at least five minutes to get the producer's home number from the secretary. By then, I'd forgotten all about Ayla

Özdal and was worrying about the phone bill, especially after the increase in telephone costs since the economic crash. Of course Petra wasn't bothered about bills or financial crashes; her hotel bill and expenses were all being paid for by the men she was trying to contact.

She dialled the number the secretary had given her. As far as I could tell, the person who answered was the producer himself.

Without allowing him to get a word in, Petra summarized that day's news in the Turkish press at lightning speed.

As you know, I hadn't seen her for years and she had never been my closest friend, but one didn't really have to know her very well or be a connoisseur of human nature like me to understand that Petra was sparing the man at the other end of the line nothing as she vented her rage.

I looked for a place where I could get away from Petra's escalating voice. The only place was the bathroom. It wasn't a luxury suite as she'd had previously, but nevertheless a luxury hotel room, a twenty-five-square-metre, tastefully furnished room.

By the time Petra had finished her conversation and was knocking on the bathroom door, I'd read the directions on all the cosmetics in the bathroom and was about to move on to the lists of ingredients.

What she told me was that Mr Franz, the German producer, had said the sacking story definitely couldn't be true; he would find out who had started that gossip and why, and call Petra back in a little while.

Actually, I found it strange that Petra had suddenly become so irate, because I'd been convinced by the impression she'd given of being unconcerned about losing her job.

"What's happened?" I asked. "Before, you didn't seem bothered that you might be sacked. Why are you so furious now?"

She picked up an envelope that had been lying on a side table and waved it under my nose.

"They gave this to me when I collected my key, didn't you notice?"

I had noticed. What's more I'd seen her biting her lip in irritation as she read the contents of that envelope in the lift but, unusually for me, I'd thought better of asking too many questions.

"Yes, I did. What does it say?" I said.

"It was sent from the production company. Mr Franz knew nothing about it. If only I knew what this Turkish producer has been up to... Apparently they're not going to pay for this room. Straight after the murder, they said the suite was too expensive and now they're saying the cost of *this* room is too high. They've found a cheaper hotel they want me to move to. Costs have shot up because of the extra time we have to spend in Istanbul and they can't meet the costs of a hotel in this price bracket..."

"Wonderful!" I thought. In that case, would she be paying for that phone call?

I thought of suggesting that Petra should move to my apartment, but immediately had second thoughts. I wasn't sure if I could bear to share my home with anyone other than Fofo just yet. The best solution would be to recommend a hotel with a view that was in my neighbourhood.

While waiting for the call from the German producer, we ordered tea from room service, knowing very well that from now on the film company would not be footing the bill.

By the time the telephone rang, I was thinking I'd have to leave if I was to make my four-o'clock appointment.

The person who called was the Turkish producer. Given that the man had abandoned his holiday to make telephone calls, Petra's call to Germany had clearly been productive.

Petra said, "One moment," in English, and passed the receiver to me.

"We can't understand each other. He doesn't know German. He speaks English but, as you know, I... You talk to him and tell me what he says."

I introduced myself to him. Right from the start, he talked to me in the familiar style of a Berlin waiter.

"Are you going to translate?" he asked.

"Yes, I am. Petra wants to know whether or not you know anything about the news that came out in the papers today."

"I've just explained to our German partner. Ayla is just trying to get herself talked about and... I mean, artists do that sort of thing to create a sensation. Miss Vogel should know all about that. Ayla took the opportunity to do it because we weren't in Istanbul. In fact there's no substance to this news ..."

I interrupted him: "You mean Ayla has some connection with your company? I don't understand what you mean."

"Madam, Ayla used to be my wife. I hope Miss Vogel will forgive us; we'll see she's compensated for this mistake."

"You mean your ex-wife started the rumour because your company was involved. Is that right?" I said, repeating what he'd said in order to be sure that I'd understood properly.

"Yes, yes, that's right. It's not important. Nothing to panic about."

I twisted my bottom lip and looked at Petra. I think it must be a Turkish trait because she didn't understand what I meant.

"But Petra had a letter from your film company today telling her to leave this hotel because they can no longer pay the bill here."

"Oh no, she doesn't have to leave. We'll sort it out when we get back to Istanbul. Make a note of my mobile number, and Miss Vogel can call us if she has any problem," he said.

After putting the telephone down, I laughed cynically. For twenty-four hours, Ayla Özdal had been discussing ridiculous conspiracy theories with various people, including homicide desk inspectors, yet it hadn't occurred to anyone that this woman might have been making it all up.

I conveyed the gist of the conversation to Petra. She calmed down considerably when she heard that the hotel fees were to be paid. With a tranquil smile, she said, "I thought there might be something like that behind Ayla Özdal's stories."

"You guessed?"

"Of course. Things like this happen all the time; remember I've been in the cinema business for twenty years. Anyway, that woman is too young; she wouldn't have been right for this part. You can't age a woman by thirty years, even with the best make-up artists."

I was annoyed with myself for not realizing the age issue before. "Yes, she's definitely too young," I murmured.

"Kurt allowed her to hope that she would have my part. He played her at her own game." Tossing her hair, she threw back her head and gave a mocking half-smile. "And anyway, who's Kurt? Who's he to sack me?"

I couldn't spend any more time learning about the tricks of people who want to be directors or film stars. It was three thirty.

I was fifteen minutes late when I entered the café opposite my shop in Kuledibi where the two reporters were drinking tea and smoking at tables covered with camera equipment. I had rushed there on foot after my conversation with the producer, Ayla Özdal's ex. There was little more I could learn from these reporters, but I didn't want to upset Lale. After all, she'd arranged for me to have a few hours with them.

The crime reporter, who I reckoned to be in his fifties, was a skinny, bald chain smoker with nicotine-stained fingers. The magazine reporter on the other hand looked young enough to be playing truant from school. They made an odd couple.

"Who's this Ayla Özdal?" I asked the youth, after the usual introductions.

"Haven't you heard of her?" he asked accusingly, as if we were talking about Claudia Cardinale. "Ayla was crowned Miss Turkey in 2000 and then went on to become a model. Three months ago she brought out an album, but it hasn't been selling very well. Apparently she's going to have a part in a new TV series due to start broadcasting next season. It was a stroke of bad luck for her that the film director was killed, because a part in an international production could have changed everything for her. What a shame, a real shame." I got the distinct impression that this young reporter was one of Ayla's admirers.

"She's supposed to have had a relationship with Mesut Mumcu. Is that true?" I asked. Mesut Mumcu was the name of the Turkish producer who had spoken to me in such a familiar manner.

"Yep, that's the rumour. Some of our colleagues saw them out together a few times... but Ayla says they're 'just friends'. I think you have to believe they're just friends unless there's proof otherwise. Things get very confused in this business. There's gossip about everyone. Why do you ask?"

"From the way Mesut *Bey* speaks about Ayla Özdal, I get the impression they were married."

The reporter found what I said amusing. He grinned and said, "In this world, relationships... It's difficult for a foreigner to understand." Perhaps he thought Germans were from another planet. I didn't disillusion him.

"Mesut *Bey* would have said that to avoid saying she's just a woman he's been sleeping with," he said, adding with a stupid grin, "Do you understand?"

"You mean they were never properly married? The man just says 'my wife' out of politeness?" I asked. Was I really from another planet?

"I don't know. Maybe they had a religious wedding ceremony. But I doubt if it was a long-standing or serious relationship. As I said, we reporters were not even sure if anything was really going on between them."

"I think I should watch a few more gossip programmes," I said, laughing.

"This business has its own code of practice," said the magazine reporter. "It's our job to provide society with information about the lives of the rich, but we don't gossip," he said emphatically.

The crime reporter nodded in agreement. A bit of professional support seemed to be required.

"There wasn't any news about the murder in the papers today. Haven't there been any new developments?" I asked. As you might have guessed, I addressed this question to the crime reporter.

"The police aren't giving anything away. I think they've been investigating something else since the murder. Mesut Mumcu was one of those released in the latest amnesty..."

As the subject moved into his field of expertise, the magazine reporter, bless him, poured out more information.

"Mesut is the former lover of Sedef Armen. They were preparing to get married at one time. In fact, Sedef had even had a wedding dress made; she was all ready to become the lady of the house, but then changed her mind. She poured out her heart to my boss Fatih, saying that after they got married Mesut wasn't going to let her work and that, after so many years of trying to get somewhere in this business, she couldn't just lose everything in one fell swoop. Fatih didn't write about all that; it would have been unprofessional to reveal the contents of a private conversation. But later, Kemal Güngör wrote about it in his column."

"Just a minute," I said, interrupting him. "Who are Fatih and Kemal Güngör?"

I think he was now convinced that I really was from another planet. In fact, I was beginning to think the same thing myself.

"Fatih is the boss of my agency. He's well known in the artistic community. And Kemal Güngör is the publishing director of the women's weekly magazine *Kadının Resmi.*"

"What do you mean by the artistic community?"

"Well, I mean artists."

I realized I was being a bit tedious but, despite my knowledge of Turkish and my razor-sharp intelligence, this magazine-speak was completely foreign to me.

"Do you mean singers, beauty queens and so forth?" I asked.

He nodded his head in an exaggerated fashion to indicate "yes".

"OK, so why did Mesut Mumcu go to jail?"

The crime reporter muttered something not very polite at the magazine reporter and took a sip of his tea before answering my question.

"He went down for a few crimes. Abduction, inciting violence, murder. He'd have been in real trouble if it hadn't been for the amnesty. It's about seven months since he got out. His gang almost broke up while he was inside, but when he came out he gathered his old team together and even managed to expand the business. For instance, he's just gone into this film business. It would've been his first film."

"Is Mesut Mumcu involved in drugs?"

I doubt if any of my readers would think I was wrong to suspect that drugs lay behind the murder of Müller. International film production costs, the fees of a big-time female film star, the expense of putting everyone up at the best hotels… A gangland boss wouldn't fund all this and go to so much trouble unless it was for some big drugs deal. And normally, a Giacomo Donetti screenplay would never be handed to someone like Kurt Müller. There was definitely something very fishy about all this.

"Mesut never does drug deals himself. His brother Aksut runs the drugs branch of the organization. They're one of the biggest families in the South-East. There are seven of them. There are some uncles too, but it's really their father who runs everything. The oldest brother, Maksut, is an MP; he's been in parliament for two terms. The sister, Yakut, is a businesswoman. You must have heard of Mumcu Tourism; they have hotels and holiday villages. Yakut's husband is German but he got himself circumcised and became a Muslim. He's been a Turkish citizen for four or five years now. He met Yakut when he came to Turkey on holiday and it was love at first sight for him. Yakut really led him along. She's a very beautiful woman. Jet-black hair, good figure, fair skin." He stopped for a moment, looking at the lad from the magazine and me. "She's quite something, she's even studied abroad."

The magazine reporter couldn't help being impressed by the in-depth knowledge of the middle-aged crime reporter. I interrupted.

"And the other three? Didn't this family produce any normal people? No housewives or teachers?"

"One of them was a favourite of the late President Turgut Özal. Damn, I've forgotten his name. Oh, what was it?" He was asking the magazine reporter who, from the way he was noisily stirring his tea and screwing up his face, clearly didn't know.

What name would parents give to their fifth child, given that they had called their other children Mesut, Aksut, Maksut and Yakut? I was about to say, "It doesn't matter," when it clicked. Even I hadn't missed the news about Turgut Mumcu's escape abroad.

"Wasn't it Turgut?" I asked.

"Yeah, of course, Turgut. He had the same name as the President. When he escaped to America, they were after him for falsified import records, faked invoices, tax evasion and stuff like that. He's probably living out his days in Miami now."

"The death of men like that is bad for our business," observed the magazine reporter.

"You said there were seven, so that leaves two. Do you know them too?" I was thinking that perhaps I ought to read the papers more often than just on Saturdays.

"Yes, there were two other siblings," he nodded. "Everyone knows their story." He addressed the magazine reporter, saying, "You know, don't you, Cumali?"

"Yeah, yeah, of course," said Cumali, but I could have sworn that he didn't.

"The two youngest were Dursun and Yeter. They were very close in age, but I think Dursun was the older one. When their brothers and sister left for Istanbul, Dursun was left in charge of the tribe. He was young, but the one who most resembled his father. I think he was intending to go into politics because he set up a large protectionist network in the area." He stopped, and then started explaining to me what a protectionist is.

"They give guns to villagers so that they can fight against terrorists…"

"I know, I know. Some of the chiefs set up state-supported people's militias," I said. Even though I didn't read the papers, I wasn't so out of touch that I didn't know what protectionists were.

"Dursun's sister Yeter had started at university in Diyarbakir. She got involved with terrorists when she was still in her first year. People say she went off to Bekaa in Lebanon. Of course it was a huge blow for the family. At first they said she'd been kidnapped, but everyone knew she'd gone of her own accord."

"How do you know so much about this family?"

"I'm from the same region, in the South-East. The family lived in the city nearest to me. I come from one of the villages around there," he said, lighting another cigarette.

"Was Yeter killed?" I asked. I had sensed the story was a tragic one and I couldn't think of a more tragic ending. He nodded his head solemnly and said, "She was badly wounded in a fight somewhere outside Diyarbakir and died a few days later. Her family went down there to collect the body for the funeral. The mother was already grieving that her daughter was a terrorist and when she got news of her death, it killed her."

"And Dursun? What happened to Dursun?"

"Dursun lost it after that. He'd go out with the men hunting terrorists in the mountains. People say he went a bit mad. It wasn't long before a terrorist's bullet got him."

For a moment, we were all silent.

"You were interested in that film director's murder, weren't you? So how did we get on to this?" said the south-eastern crime reporter.

"Because of Mesut Mumcu's drugs links," I said.

"Oh yes. As I said, Aksut looks after the drugs business."

"Is that something everyone knows about?" I asked.

"How would everyone know about it?" said the crime reporter.

Clearly we were getting to a point where both reporters were starting to become cagey.

"I don't mean… I'm just talking generally."

"Of course, it's no secret. We don't write about it in the papers, but we know who's involved in what."

"You said the police were being very secretive about this investigation. Why is that, do you think? I mean, is there something unusual about it?"

He didn't reply immediately. He twirled his plastic lighter between his thumb and forefinger, leaned forwards and asked the waiter for three more teas.

"When our boss said a friend of Lale Hanım wanted to talk to a reporter about the film director's murder, I thought it couldn't be just an everyday murder… There's… how would you say, there's something different about it?"

"Something incongruous?" I suggested.

He looked up from the lighter he was fiddling with, glanced at me and said, "Where did you learn your Turkish?"

"I was born in Istanbul and lived here until I was seven. I've also been living here for the last thirteen years."

"Your name's foreign, so…" he said, clearly unsure what to make of me.

"So, there's something incongruous about this murder…" I said, trying to get back to what we had been discussing.

"Why are you so interested in it? The homicide desk is behaving strangely to be sure. They usually give us more information, but they haven't even told us properly how the murder was committed. All they said was that someone threw a hair-dryer into the water when the man was having a bath."

"But you have police contacts you can ask for information."

"At the moment, that's the problem. When the boss told me to be here at four o'clock, I called an old friend from back home, thinking I'd get some information. He's a policeman himself. I asked him if he knew anything and promised not to write about it. But this investigation is clearly being conducted at a high level. Even the cops have no idea what's going on. It's strange. What's so secret about it? My friend said there were certain constraints. The murder victim is German, so the Germans want their own people to be in the investigation team. The suspects are also German, that is to say one of the film crew might have murdered him. If they go back home, they can't be arrested. It all needs to be sorted out quickly, or at the very least they need to find some sound evidence."

"Hmm," I murmured. If they were taking this business so seriously, Batuhan had taken a big risk by gadding about with me at the kebab restaurant.

At my insistence, I paid for the teas and rose to go back to the shop. We shook hands and the crime reporter said he would let me know if he heard anything. He wrote my name and the shop telephone number on his cigarette packet. I nodded my appreciation.

The café where I'd met the reporters was only two minutes away from the shop. When I went in, Pelin was working away at the computer.

"Hello," I said.

"Hi," she replied brightly.

"Working hard, are you?"

"All the shop records were in such a mess. The incoming invoices, outgoing invoices, cheques and cash payments just didn't add up. I just thought I'd spend some time taking care of the paperwork."

She had emphasized the words "some time", but I had no idea what she meant.

"Have there been any calls?"

"Loads." She got up and slung her bag over her back. "Anyway, I'm off. I'll open up the shop tomorrow. Take a look over the books if you have time. I've left a list of who called on the table."

Without giving me time to even say "See you later", she disappeared. The air conditioning had been working continuously all day, making the air inside the shop very heavy. I took the risk of opening the door and letting in some sticky heat.

My Australian friend Cindy had rung for some reason, but what really interested me was seeing Sandra's name on the list; Sandra, the retired doctor in Kurt Müller's home town.

I went straight to the telephone.

I had just taken a deep breath, ready to leave a voicemail after the fourth ring, when I was surprised to hear Sandra answering in person. "Sandra," was all I could say.

"Kati! You got my message very quickly," she replied, in that weary tone that only retired people have.

I had no idea what she meant by "very quickly". Trying not to think about the cost of calls between Turkey and Germany, I asked, "Did you manage to find out anything?"

"I certainly did, and I enjoyed myself. Let me know if you have any more detective work that needs doing. I feel like Jessica Fletcher."

Good, I had brought a little excitement into the life of my retired friend.

"OK, so what did you learn?"

"Well, as you know, Müller is a very common name. So I thought there was no point going through the telephone directory. I called my son's friend Reinhard, who works for *Bielefeld Post*, our local paper. He'd heard nothing about a murder victim called Müller. The man's hardly a Wim Wenders after all. Hallo!! Hallo, Kati!"

"I'm here, I'm listening to you," I said.

"Oh, I thought we were cut off. The connection's not very good, there's a bad echo. The sound quality has really deteriorated since privatization. Anyway, Reinhard phoned Müller's family, saying that he was writing an article. A man gave him the mother's rest home address. However, the woman is very old and couldn't talk very well. She's probably senile. Apparently Müller has a younger brother living in Düsseldorf who agreed to meet Reinhard. I asked what his job was. And you'll like this, he's actually a surgeon. What's more, he's my brother's senior consultant. I thought such coincidences only happened in films." She took a breath and let out a loud laugh. I think Sandra had just lived the most exciting two days since her retirement.

"I called my brother Detlev straight away. He was really surprised to hear my voice. We see each other so rarely, especially since Mother died. You haven't met his wife. It's his third, and she's twenty-five years younger than Detlev. It's not right…"

"Sandra!"

"Oh yes, yes. What was I saying? Oh yes, I called Detlev and asked him to get me an appointment with Mr Müller. As an ordinary patient. Naturally, I said nothing to my brother about the murder. Since I didn't know Müller's specialist field, I just invented an illness. But Detlev insisted he had a neurologist friend who's a better surgeon and said he'd fix up an appointment for me with him. That friend is Turkish, and I know you like Turks. Detlev told me the man's name, but I've forgotten it. I'll find it out for you if you want, if you still…"

The loneliness of old people in Germany certainly makes them talkative. "Sandra!" I repeated, in a warning tone of voice. She was definitely talking too much.

"OK, OK. Anyway, Detlev arranged an appointment with Müller for me this morning at ten o'clock. I drove to Düsseldorf, which as you know isn't far. Mr Müller is quite young, thirty-five at the most. He met me personally at the door, thanks to Detlev of course. I told him straight away that I too was a doctor in order to establish a bit of closeness, and then I told him about you. The poor young man hadn't a clue what I was talking about until I mentioned Istanbul, and then he looked very strange. I quickly explained that I wasn't ill and that you had asked me to do some research on his brother, which was why I'd made the appointment. He looked worried and I immediately realized that he was anxious because of Detlev. 'Young man,' I said, 'everyone except us thinks this is an ordinary thirty-minute medical appointment. It has nothing to do with anyone else.' He relaxed then."

"So, what did you learn, Sandra?"

"You don't let me get a word in edgeways." She paused for a moment. She'd said so many irrelevant things that she had confused herself.

"What did I learn? Mr Müller said he hadn't seen his older brother for a long time. They'd more or less lost touch. Apparently this young surgeon was paying all the costs of their mother's care home; his older brother Kurt was a good-for-nothing. I asked him what his brother did. He said he'd made some stupid films. They last met twelve years ago, when Kurt asked if he could stay with him for a while. Our surgeon friend reckoned that Kurt was in serious trouble, otherwise why would he want to stay in his brother's student flat, because normally he had plenty of money to throw about. However, our surgeon didn't let him stay and hadn't heard anything of his brother since, until he saw press reports of his death. Kurt didn't even go to see their mother in the care home. Mr Müller said he didn't want his name associated with that of his brother."

"Is that all?" I asked, feeling disappointed.

"That's all," said Sandra.

"Didn't he have any close friends? Did you ask if there was anyone else we could contact?"

"Yes, I asked him that as well, but Mr Müller doesn't know of anyone. I asked him who his brother's friends were when he was at school in Bielefeld, and he said his closest school friend was Günter Basile."

"Is this man still in Bielefeld? Do you know him?"

"What do you mean, do I know him? The whole of Germany knows him. Do you still not read the papers?"

I chose to ignore the last remark. "Who's this Basile?"

"He's the number-two man in the Liberal Democrats…"

"And former defence minister, I remember now," I said.

"Yes, in the last government. But I doubt if a successful politician would meet you or me to rake over memories of a long-forgotten childhood friend."

"Hmm," I said.

Sandra hadn't come up with anything.

I walked home, changed into my favourite pink shorts and a T-shirt with a Donald Duck motif that I'd bought from a surplus stall at the local Tuesday market, and started making a mushroom omelette. I realized I was inviting trouble by eating eggs in that heat, but I couldn't be bothered to think about health. Anyway, I needed to punish myself for being unable to set aside all this detective work, and concentrate on my mounting telephone bills and neglected shop accounts.

I was lying on the sofa picking at the omelette and some week-old lettuce leaves when the doorbell rang. It was eight twenty-five.

I bent down and crept to the window to see who was at the door. No one was there. Some local children must have rung the bell and run away.

I had just settled myself on the sofa again when the doorbell rang a second time. This time, I went straight to the door and, sounding like a sensible woman living alone, called out, "Who's there?"

"Batuhan." I have to say that the sound of his voice gave me more pleasure than if it had been my favourite tenor in *Il trovatore*.

I simply have to describe to my dear readers what I saw when I opened the door. Batuhan was wearing ordinary tight-fitting jeans, a claret-coloured polo shirt with a green crocodile on his left breast, and claret-coloured espadrilles on his feet. For me, it wasn't just the fact that they were claret-coloured, but that all production of espadrilles was supposed to have been banned by a special decree of the Council of Ministers. It was inconceivable that anyone in a senior position in the service of the state would go for espadrilles.

To complete the picture, Batuhan was carrying a briefcase in his hand. At least that wasn't claret-coloured.

"I didn't know your home phone number, so I couldn't call you. Anyway, when I dropped you off at home last night, I wasn't as drunk as I thought, so I remembered the way. Are you alone?"

"I had the Berlin Philharmonic here, but they've gone now," I said. As soon as I spoke, I was horrified at my bad joke. However, either Batuhan was used to bad jokes or he laughed to humour me. A third possibility also occurred to me, which was that he didn't know what the Berlin Philharmonic was, but I didn't want to admit that, even to myself.

"Come in," I said. He was still standing outside the door.

I plunged back into the living room to hide the unappetizing and pathetic-looking plate of omelette and salad lying on the sofa before Batuhan entered. We had become quite at ease with each other by the end of the previous night's meal and bottle of *rakı*. Nevertheless, being on familiar terms did not mean he needed to know how and where I ate when I wasn't eating kebabs. I kicked the plate firmly under the sofa and called out to Batuhan, who was now standing in the entrance hall.

"Won't you sit down?"

He stopped at the door of the living room, opened his briefcase and took out two bottles of wine. I desperately wanted to remark, "I hope those aren't claret as well." But I controlled myself.

"I brought some wine. You'll have a drink, won't you?"

"Sure," I said.

He followed me as I went to the kitchen to get a corkscrew.

"Has there been any progress in the investigation?" I asked.

He didn't answer, but sat on the chair next to the kitchen door watching me struggle with the cork.

"I'll open it if you like," he said finally.

I passed the bottle and corkscrew to him, took out some wineglasses and put them on the kitchen worktop.

"Not much is happening," he said. He was obviously not referring to his difficulty separating the cork from the wine bottle. "A lot of pressure is being put on us. It makes me sick."

He spoke as if we'd been friends for forty years. I leaned my chin on my hand and looked at him thoughtfully. He was busy with the bottle and didn't see the expression on my face.

"Why is there all this pressure? It's a murder investigation, and you're an inspector on the homicide desk. You do this sort of investigation every day."

He shrugged his shoulders. "Yes, but the murder victim and suspects are foreign citizens. The German police want to get involved. I'm being pressured from above to solve the case as quickly as possible without letting them in. So far the Germans haven't got the necessary clearance, but who knows what'll happen tomorrow," he said wearily.

"My theory about the murder…" Before I could finish my sentence, he stood and picked up the briefcase that he'd kept close by him and the wine bottle.

"Shall we go into the living room?" he asked.

"Are we going to talk about the murder?" I asked, sitting on the sofa with a wineglass in one hand and a cigarette in the other. I was getting tired of playing cat-and-mouse.

"Yes, we are. There are a few things I want to ask you."

"I had no connection with it. Why are you asking me questions?"

"It's not because you had any connection with it. I just want to ask you some questions," he said.

I imagined my new visiting card:

Kati Hirschel
Bookseller-Detective
Murder Consultant

"I'll answer your questions if you give me details of how the murder was committed," I said, well aware that my words had a whiff of blackmail but, as you know, sometimes you have to resort to dubious methods to get what you want.

With an openness that surprised me, Batuhan started to explain without any hesitation.

"Because the body was in water, it's impossible to determine what time the murder took place. After the crew had dinner together that night, five of them stayed out, including Müller. They all returned to the hotel and got into the same lift at around eleven forty. The rooms of Müller, his assistant director Miss Bauer and production assistant Mr Gust were on the fourth floor. Those three came out of the lift together. Gust realized that Müller was very drunk and offered to take him to his room, or rather his suite. On that floor there are two suites on the Bosphorus side of the hotel, with good views. On the other side, the street side, they're all rooms. Müller declined the offer, so Gust and Bauer went to their rooms on the street side and Müller went off in the opposite direction. In other words, they separated as soon as they came out of the lift. Those two were the last people to see Müller alive. According to their statements, they spent the night together in Miss Bauer's room."

He stopped for a moment to take a sip of wine.

"Had Bauer and Gust previously been having a relationship? Or was that the first time?…"

"They said they got it together for the first time that night over dinner. Of course, the man's married. They drank a lot and spent the night together."

"Their rooms were next door to each other, which is too much of a coincidence if they weren't having an affair. Which of the film crew allocated the rooms, and how?"

"The room reservations were made before they arrived in Istanbul. They'd booked eleven single rooms and two suites. But it wasn't clear beforehand who was to stay in which room. Reception had allocated randomly. The suites… Well there were two suite reservations. The two suites in the hotel were next to each other and had been booked for the film crew, or rather for Müller and his friend Miss Vogel. As for Bauer and Gust's rooms being next door to each other," he said scratching his head, "that was coincidence of course."

"That's a very big coincidence, Batuhan," I said sardonically. Contrary to what I thought, my manner did not offend Batuhan's masculine pride. He took out a notebook from the briefcase, and jotted something down.

"You're saying Müller came out of the lift at eleven forty and was last seen alive walking towards his room."

"Yes, and the body was found at five twenty."

"It is true that he was murdered in the bath, isn't it?"

"Do you think we, the Turkish police, are the sort of people to joke about such things?"

Actually, I'd never felt less like laughing.

"That left less than six hours. If he hadn't been killed, he would have started that day with five hours' sleep. If I'd been in that situation, I'd have gone straight to bed rather than indulge in a bath. All the others said he was drunk, except for those two... What were their names?"

"Bauer and Gust. But there was no need for anyone to say whether he was drunk or not, because the autopsy made it clear that he had a high blood-alcohol count."

"Hmm," I said, deep in thought. Clearly, Müller hadn't been burned to a cinder by being electrocuted as I'd expected. There was a body on which an autopsy could be carried out.

"It seems odd to me that someone who was drunk would go and have a bath instead of going straight to bed."

"Getting into it with a whisky glass is even stranger," he said.

"He had a whisky glass in his hand?" I stopped. "In his hand? What do you mean? In the bath?"

"No, in his hand. He was clutching the glass very tightly."

"How?" First his body turned out not to have been burned to toast, and now this.

"In the case of sudden or traumatic death, the muscles in the lower arms, especially the hands, remain contracted instead of slackening. Haven't you ever seen war photos showing dead people with flags in their hands, who apparently died for the flag and with the flag clutched in their hand?"

Without responding to Batuhan's last sentence, I grimaced and said, "In the bath, with a whisky glass stuck in his hand... Poor man."

Suddenly I had an idea. "So, any suspicion of suicide was eliminated because he had a whisky glass in his hand?" I said. As I said this, I thought about the reaction of the wardrobe mistress who had been the first person to see the body.

Batuhan responded to this, saying, "Suicide never even occurred to us because of the position of the body."

"Fine, but didn't he try to save himself?"

"There was no chance of escaping death in such circumstances. Again, because of the muscles. You remember how I said the hands and forearms remain contracted? Well, there is involuntary contraction of the other muscles in the body as well. It would have been absolutely impossible for him to get out of the water."

"OK, so what state was the body in?"

"What do you mean, what state was it in?"

"Well, I thought when people were subjected to an electric shock, they were burned to a cinder, but, according to what you said, that was not the case."

"Yes, a normal electric shock would turn a body to charcoal."

"You mean if you put your finger into an electric socket..."

He carried on as if he hadn't heard what I said:

"In water… because water is a good conductor… Death takes place because the heart stops." It seemed to me that he didn't know much about this either.

"Hmm," I said again. Actually, I was more interested in the state of the hair-dryer than the body. "I want to ask you something else."

"Ask away."

"About the hair-dryer. In hotels, hair-dryers are usually made so that they won't work unless you keep pressing the button down, as a safety measure. Anyway, I won't generalize, but the hair-dryers in that hotel worked on that basis. Did the murderer put the dryer into the water while pressing the button?"

He nodded at me approvingly. "Did you check the hair-dryers at the hotel?" he asked.

"I looked at the one in Petra's room and assumed they all worked the same way." I hadn't only been studying the instructions and ingredients of anti-wrinkle creams while I was in Petra's bathroom that morning.

"You're right," he said. "They're the same in all the rooms, including Müller's. You have to keep the button pressed for it to work. But the murderer didn't use the hotel hair-dryer."

"What!" I exclaimed.

"It was a cheap and simple model, produced by Philips about four years ago and no longer on the market. The company made those products in Taiwan. They made millions of them and sold them all over the world… Unfortunately, the same model was on sale in Turkey and Germany. We've been unable to get anywhere along that trail."

"And that model had a very long electric cord…" I said. He looked at me so strangely, I felt obliged to explain why I had said such a thing:

"As you know, Petra was staying in a suite. In that suite, the bathroom alone was almost the size of my living room." As I said this, Batuhan let his eyes wander round the living room as if trying to measure its size. I continued to explain my theory:

"I don't actually know where the socket was in the bathroom, but if we assume that, like most sockets, it was near the washbasin, there was quite a distance between the socket and the bath." I was tired of repeating the word "socket".

I considered whether or not my words made sense, and added, "That is if the suites are all the same size."

"They are the same size," he said, nodding his head. "You've actually thought things through very well. But you're not the only one to think of that; the murderer also thought about it because he or she brought along some extension leads. Three cables, two metres long each... Two were attached to each other, the other was unused."

"You mean that the murderer was standing there fixing extension leads together while Müller was drinking whisky in the bath? Oh, that's just rubbish!"

"They probably weren't fixed together in the bathroom. It's most likely that he or she prepared them in the living room while Müller was in the bath. We found the unused cable on the table in the living room."

"Hmm," I said. "And there weren't any fingerprints on the cables?"

"None," he said, with a sigh. He had clearly hoped there would be, until the results of the laboratory analysis arrived. "It's pointless looking for fingerprints in hotel rooms so we don't usually bother about them.

However, this time, we checked the whisky bottle, the socket and the cables. It's as if the murderer wore gloves, which is ridiculous. The murder victim would obviously have been suspicious of someone wandering around wearing gloves. But there wasn't a single fingerprint on the extension leads."

"Maybe the murder victim didn't have time to get suspicious," I said.

"Unlikely. The murderer would have opened the door quietly, entered and fixed the leads together while Müller was in the bath... Anyway, how did the murderer know that Müller would be in the bath? What made him or her think of entering the room to commit a murder with a hair-dryer? Also, there was no sign of the door being forced."

"The fact that the murder weapon was a hair-dryer complicates things, doesn't it? If Müller had been killed by a gun like everyone else, we wouldn't be thinking about all this," I said. There was a short silence. I sat smoking and making smoke rings. I realized my face looked ridiculous as I did it but, as you will appreciate, I was way past the age of worrying about such things.

"Even if it wasn't Petra, I think the murderer was a woman," he said, looking at my funny expression out of the corner of his eye.

"That's because everything bad in the world is brought about by women, isn't it?" I exclaimed. I had of course noticed the previous night that he was a bit hesitant about Petra being the murderer.

Batuhan leaned over and looked at me. What I saw was a picture of an aggrieved-looking policeman.

"I'll tell you why I think that. What keeps bothering me is that Müller undressed and got into the bath while someone was there. If it had been a man, he wouldn't have undressed and got into the bath, would he?" He stopped and then answered the question that was forming in his mind.

"All right, he might have been gay, but we're not at all sure about that. One of his closest friends was in the film crew, and from his statements…" He wasn't satisfied with what he had just said, but I didn't pursue it.

"I think there was a woman in the room and that Müller was having a relationship with her," he continued eagerly. "He probably didn't have sexual relations with a woman that night, because there was no trace of it. The bed wasn't disturbed and, well, we didn't find any used condoms… But as I said, if he was naked in the presence of another man…"

I interrupted him, saying, "I've heard that Turkish men show each other their penises and measure them with a ruler. Is that a lie?"

"We're not talking about young boys here," he said, as if young boys didn't one day turn into grown men.

If I hadn't spent the first seven and last thirteen years of my life in Istanbul, I would never have been able to understand the meaning that lay behind what he said. Batuhan was a product of a community in which men roam around a male *hamam* in loincloths, and women wear knickers in theirs; they do not take them off even to wash. Müller, on the other hand, came from Germany, where people wander naked at mixed-sex saunas, naturist beaches and swimming pools – facilities that exist nowhere else in the world apart from a few northern countries. I'd never met Müller, but I guessed it was not only when he was little that he showed his penis to male friends.

"What you said might be valid for Turks, but there's no such taboo about nudity in Germany. What I mean is that people don't only undress for sex or when they're with people they're having sex with. If someone opens the door to the postman with nothing on, that postman doesn't immediately think they're offering themselves to him. There are even nude sunbathing sections at public swimming pools in some neighbourhoods. It's a cultural difference."

He gaped at me, saying, "Are you serious? Do you mean a grown man, who's not homosexual, would strip and get into a bath in front of another man?"

"Of course he would, no doubt about it."

Batuhan looked at me despairingly. If the clues that made them think Petra or some other woman had committed the murder were so flaky, then he and his colleagues really had their work cut out.

"Yesterday, Ayla Özdal announced at a press conference that she was to be given Petra's part," I said. There was nothing exclusive about the information I'd been given the previous night.

He pursed his lips. "I'm not sure if what Ayla said last night was true. We took her statement today and I think she's been telling blatant lies. Something may have been going on between Müller and this Ayla, or she may just have been after a bit of self-publicity."

Again, there was silence. We were both deep in thought.

"There's something I'd really like to ask you," I said in my most appealing voice.

"Go ahead."

"Didn't the electricity cut out when the hair-dryer was thrown into the bath? I mean, wouldn't the fuses have blown?"

"They would and they did."

"Did the murderer bring a flashlight? How did he or she find the way down the corridor?"

"The rooms have separate fuses. It's true, the fuse in Müller's suite did blow. But that means nothing. The corridor lights were on when the murderer left the suite. Even if he or she had taken a light, it would only have been used as far as the door of the suite. If the fuses for the whole floor or the whole hotel had blown, the murder might have been discovered earlier."

"OK, but who told you that Petra and Müller were having a relationship?"

"Ask me who didn't say that. Just about everyone in the film crew knew. It was the first thing they said when they made their statements. There was just one woman in the film crew who said it couldn't have been happening. Apart from her, everyone was certain about it."

"Did you ask Petra if they were having a relationship?"

"I asked her yesterday when she came into the police station. She said 'definitely not'. And this afternoon when I questioned her, she said the whole idea was rubbish and there was definitely nothing going on."

Batuhan continued his explanation.

"The film crew talked about a big stormy love affair. So it was strange that Petra denied it so vehemently." He ran his hand through his hair. "We haven't uncovered any real motive. Yet, when you think about it, who would Müller open the door to so late at night when he was due to get up very early the next morning? Who would he miss out on sleep for?…"

"Only for his lover," I said.

We sat for a while without saying anything. I thought about what we'd discussed, then suddenly snapped my fingers as I had an idea.

"I've got it," I said. "Have you checked on the extension lead that was attached to the dryer? Where were the leads bought?"

"Bravo. You didn't even miss that," he said, half teasingly, half admiringly. I couldn't work out which way he was most inclined.

"Well?" I said, waiting for a response.

"The leads were better quality than those produced in Turkey. But although they weren't Turkish-made, leads of that quality are found in several shops here."

"So the leads don't get us anywhere then."

He shook his head.

"I can see the bottom of the wine bottle," he said. "I'll open the other one."

"Let's go out, if you feel like it. I'm hungry. We could eat toasted cheese at the Bambi *Büfe*. At this hour…" – I looked at the clock – "It's ten past ten. We've got time to digest it before bedtime."

"Fine."

"In that case, I'll just change," I said, setting off towards the bedroom in my 1,600-square-foot apartment.

As I was opening the wardrobe door, I realized it was the first time in ages that I wasn't feeling uncomfortable in the heat that night. It wasn't because the evenings had got cooler, although it would have been a blessing if they had. My mind was so busy with the murder that I wasn't bothered by the weather. I hadn't even thought about Fofo for the last two days. Realizing that, I felt a pang. How could I ever forget about Fofo?

As my anger at and love for Fofo battled with each other in my heart, I felt a sudden need to take care of myself, to make up for the way I treated my poor body: I would wear something smart.

I have to admit that my reasons for dressing up were not merely to reward myself.

I put on my favourite tight-fitting green skirt and a grey shirt that buttoned down the front. These were complemented with a pair of flat sandals decorated with large metal rings on top, and a dab of perfume. My hair adorned my head like a masterfully crafted crown of rare jewels: I was satisfied with my reflection in the mirror.

So was Batuhan.

I was just as aware as you, my dear readers, that it was not the most appropriate outfit for eating toasted cheese sandwiches at a stand-up eatery, but I couldn't have cared less.

After we'd eaten our toast, we went to a club on the Bosphorus where the underclasses wiggle their hips and wave their arms, belly-dancing until dawn to throbbing Turkish music. Before long, I felt as if my head was about to explode from the noise and my eyes would never again see the beauty of the Bosphorus, so I suggested we leave. Batuhan insisted on dropping me off at home as his car was parked close to my apartment.

When we reached the door of the apartment block, I invited him in for coffee out of politeness.

"I have to come in anyway because I left my bag at your place," he said brazenly. I hadn't noticed the absence of that awful briefcase, either when we were eating toast or afterwards. That's why I was first surprised and then angry that his bag was lying on my sofa. He'd left it there so that he would have an excuse to come up if I didn't invite him in. Typical eastern cunning. I suddenly wanted to say, "No need to come up. I'll lower it down from the window in the shopping basket."

Yet, he didn't deserve that... He hadn't really done anything so awful.

We went up together.

He was trying to stretch my skirt and get his leg in between my legs. The skirt was very tight. My body was pressed against his and, as he started to stroke my hip, I let out an involuntary squeal of desire.

"Disgraceful... Having sex with a policeman, it's disgraceful!" I thought. Furthermore, I felt I was betraying my mother. The only thing we shared in life as mother and daughter was a hatred of the police...

Such thoughts quickly evaporated. He was bearing down on my left hip joint with a firmness that made me want him like crazy. I felt his large dark hand pushing up my skirt while the other caressed my breast through my shirt.

"Shall we go to the bedroom?" I whispered.

"Why?" he asked.

"Come on," I said, disregarding his policeman's fantasies.

He didn't reply, but he also didn't move.

I heard the sound of the silk-covered buttons of my shirt dropping one by one onto the stone floor of the passage and wondered how he was going to undo my bra. Would it be with the dexterity of experience, or the excitement of a novice?

He didn't undo my bra.

He pulled aside the bra and exposed my breasts, then pulled my shirtsleeves and bra straps over my elbows. I couldn't move my arms very easily; in fact I couldn't really move at all – all my energy had evaporated. "Paralysed by desire," I thought. My clitoris was aching to be touched. I wanted his dark hand to find the place between my legs that was on fire, but my skirt, my long tight skirt, prevented his hand from going where I wanted it.

My back was against the cold white wall; the sleeves of my blouse and my supposedly elastic bra straps trapped my upper arms... Because I couldn't move, couldn't guide him in any way, couldn't undo his trouser zip, couldn't push his hand to where I wanted it to go, or maybe because I couldn't pull up my own long tight skirt, whatever the reason, I felt a sudden need to escape from my lustful torpor, and more importantly from the control he had over me, so I repeated, "Let's go to the bedroom."

"Shhhh!" he said.

As I heard the sound of a zip being undone, I leaned my head on his shoulder and looked down. With his trousers round his legs, he pulled down his white cotton underpants with one hand. In the light that filtered into the passage through the open balcony door, I saw his dark hard penis and I wanted it inside me like mad. He pulled up my skirt until it was gathered round my waist; he held me by my hips and, with my back against the wall, lifted me up as easily as if I were a rag doll. With my legs entwined around his hips, I couldn't move my arms or my body, which was squashed between the wall and his penis, but despite every organ in my body desiring the superiority he exercised over me, I was seized with anger and an unreasonable obstinacy.

"I don't want to," I almost shouted.

"What?" he said. Tenderly, he pushed my hair away from my forehead.

"You heard. I don't want to. Put me down," I said.

He didn't say another word and put me down. Silently, he pulled up his underpants and his trousers that were around my ankles.

He didn't say, "What happened?" He didn't ask, "Why?"

I tugged my skirt down and tried to fasten my shirt buttons, then realized they were no longer there. My heart started pounding again. A moment ago it had been pumping blood down to my groin; now the blood was rushing upwards to my brain. I turned away from him and went to the bedroom. Dazzled by the ceiling light, I put on the first T-shirt that came to hand in the drawer of the wardrobe.

"Would you like some coffee?" I said, as I walked from the bedroom to the kitchen without looking at him. He was still standing motionless in the passage, where he had just done up his zip. He looked at his watch.

"It's nearly one o'clock," he murmured.

"So?" I said.

"A beer would be better than coffee."

"What happens if a policeman is caught driving after drinking?" I asked, kneeling down to search for a beer in the depths of a kitchen cupboard.

"Policeman? You mean if an inspector is caught," he corrected me. "They'd say: so sorry, sir, didn't recognize you, sir."

"You're not serious," I said.

"Of course I'm serious. Have you ever heard of an inspector losing his driving licence because of drink driving?"

"No, I haven't. But that doesn't count, because you're the only inspector I know," I said, trying to stand up. "There's no beer in the house, but I have some wine if you want."

"A German without beer in the house is like a football team without a manager," he said.

There was no point in asking what he meant because it was clearly just a police joke. I understood then that the tension of a little while ago would not affect our relationship, and he wouldn't ask me why I hadn't wanted him.

6

I woke up with a dreadful migraine in the right side of my head. It was so early that I wouldn't have normally been awake even if I'd set my alarm. I went into the shower and massaged my shoulders under the hot water. Afterwards, I went out onto the balcony with a large cup of strong Turkish coffee. But the coffee made me feel shaky, so I waited patiently for the local shop to open at eight o'clock. I had nothing to eat at home and I didn't want to take migraine tablets on an empty stomach.

Vans delivered trays of golden newly baked bread and piles of newspapers to the doorway of the corner shop. The grocer's boy, Hamdi, sprinkled handfuls of water on the ground from a plastic bucket to keep down the dust, turning it to mud. He then started to sweep the ground with a coarse twig brush. Was it coarse, or was it the way Hamdi did it? To decide, I held out against the migraine and stood at the window for a while watching him. In the end, I decided there was no answer.

"Hamdii! Hamdiii!" I called out in a loud whisper.

He raised his head and our eyes met.

"Hey, Kati! You're up early this morning. Do you want all the papers again today?" Without waiting for a reply, he ran into the shop for scissors to cut the nylon tape that bound the piles of papers.

When he came back, I called him again, "Hamdiii! There's a list in the basket. I need bread as well."

"OK, miss, straight away." He turned towards the shopping basket I lowered from the window, with surprising agility for a lad of his size.

I rested my elbows on the window sill and settled down to wait for Hamdi to fetch the things on my list. Two minutes later, he was at the shop door again.

"Miss, we've run out of blackberry jelly. There's quince and raspberry. Which would you like?" he shouted out at the top of his voice. Thinking of my neighbours trying to sleep, I motioned to him to keep his voice down, hauled the basket back up and put on my slippers to go to the shop.

I'd been taking migraine tablets after breakfast ever since Fofo had left. Despite the coffee, I closed the bedroom curtains and went back to bed in the hope that I might sleep for another half-hour.

When I woke up, the sun was high and I had fully recovered from the migraine.

I sat in the kitchen waiting for the kettle to boil and looking at the front pages of the newspapers: the effects of the economic crisis that had burst on us in February had not gone away. There had been protest marches against increases in the cost of living in various parts of the country. Two MPs were roughed up when they asked people to be reasonable on a visit to Elmadağ, a district of Yozgat; one of them was taken to Yozgat State Hospital.

I wondered whether this resistance to the rising cost of living might actually topple this Turkish regime that had survived every kind of political scandal and corruption.

As I poured the tea, I noticed a photograph on page three of Lale's newspaper. It was a picture of Fofo's former lover, the lawyer in the cravat. This piece of low-life was standing next to an extremely attractive man, and they were both surrounded by police. I glanced at the headline – "Gangland Producer Caught at Home Partying with Lover" – and found myself willing this lover to be our cravat-wearing lawyer.

Police have a new suspect for the murder of the German film director that took place in the early hours of Monday morning in the Hotel Bosphorus, *one of Istanbul's grandest establishments.*

In a move worthy of a movie thriller, famous gangland boss Mesut Mumcu was caught early yesterday evening with his sixteen-year-old lover A.K. at his magnificent mini-palace near Kavakdibi in Fethiye, where they had been living it up for days out of the public gaze. He was asked to make a statement in connection with the investigation into the murder of German film director Kurt Müller.

While Müller was taking a bath in the Dolmabahçe suite of the Hotel Bosphorus, *where former American President Bill Clinton recently stayed with his wife and daughter, an electric hair-dryer was thrown into the bathwater, creating an electric current that instantly killed the German film director. Mesut Mumcu, producer of the film* A Thousand and One Nights in the Harem, *has been sought for several days by the police who have wanted to take a statement from him.*

Mesut Mumcu was previously tried for the crime of forming a gang for criminal purposes, but acquitted on grounds of insufficient evidence.

Mumcu has spent time in jail for crimes such as hiring killers, abduction and intent to murder. When his last sentence was suspended under the Amnesty Law, he set up the Mumcu Film Company and went into the film-production business.

It was noted that his lawyer was present when Mumcu got into the police vehicle that took him to Istanbul to make his statement.

It was difficult to make sense of this article, but it quickly became clear that Fofo's former lover, the lawyer Ali Vardar, was not Mesut Mumcu's lover but his lawyer. If that was the case, Ali Vardar had the chance to make up for his scumbag life by being useful: he could tell me what he knew about his client.

I felt a thrill of excitement as I dialled Ali Vardar's number, which I'd found in an old phone book; however, I still had no idea what my strategy was going to be.

The woman who answered the phone sounded as if she wanted to be included in the annual poll of Turkey's most sexy women. I asked to speak to Mr Vardar.

"You've called the wrong number, sweetie. This is his home not his office. Call the office," she said, and put the phone down.

I dialled the same number again.

"Madam, I'm İsmail Yurdakul's secretary. If you have Mr Vardar's office number, would you mind giving it to me?" I asked.

It was irrelevant who İsmail Yurdakul was or whether he was someone of any importance. However, being addressed as "madam", especially by a secretary, would make her drop her aggressive tone and melt like butter, trash that she was. If it worked, this was the quickest way of finding Ali Vardar's office number.

"İsmail Yurdakul?"

I had expected her to say, "And who is he?" or at the very least, "You asked to speak to Mr Vardar a moment ago." As it was, there was no need to overrate the woman's intelligence, because this unpleasant little scene didn't take place.

"Ali's office number is 2937347," she said, and put the phone down again.

In view of the woman's ability to memorize this number, it seemed that Ali had changed his sexual preference and found someone suited to his class and clientele.

When I dialled the office number, a competent-sounding voice told me that Mr Vardar was out and would not return before six o'clock, so I should phone later.

I made my way through the narrow streets of Çukurcuma, using my years of experience to avoid any serious danger. As I walked, I didn't think about the Kurt Müller murder or about Batuhan. I thought about Bellini, composer of *La sonnambula*, who died at the age of thirty-four. When I say I thought about him, I hadn't the slightest idea what he looked like or what kind of person he was, I just thought what a shame it was that he had died at the age of thirty-four. Turkish politics was full of so many useless people; why did Bellini have to die instead of one of them?

I finally decided that reading newspapers was having a negative effect on me. All that news about corruption, shameless politicians and dicey businessmen was depressing me.

As I sat alone in the coolness of the shop's air conditioning, drinking gallons of tea while I waited for customers, I couldn't stop thinking about Bellini and Turkish politicians – it was a badly timed obsession.

This time, I saw Batuhan before *cayci* Recai did. It was a little after three o'clock. Unfortunately, he was in plain clothes again. He gave a cursory glance at the books in the window and came in.

"Hello," he said, distantly and absent-mindedly, holding out his hand to shake hands as if nothing had happened between us. I began to think there was something mentally wrong with Batuhan. Was he actually being mature and tolerant about what had happened the previous night?

"Hello," I said, thinking as I extended my hand that it was time I went for a manicure. What a thankless task all this physical grooming was.

I set aside my thoughts about Bellini, my nails and Turkish politicians, and tried to concentrate on Batuhan.

"You're in plain clothes again today," I said, for something to say.

"I always wear plain clothes."

"What do you mean 'always'? When we first met, you were in uniform."

"There was an official meeting at the station that day and I had to be in uniform. I normally wear plain clothes."

"Hmmm," I said.

I wanted to change the subject, so I said, "I see you've arrested Mesut Mumcu."

"Yes, they arrested him."

"Aren't you handling that investigation?"

"When it's an ordinary murder, I take care of it. Otherwise it goes to Organized Crime. At the moment we're squabbling over it, but it looks as if I'll lose." His manner was perfectly normal as he pulled up a chair and sat down. I was just about to open my mouth to speak when his mobile rang.

Batuhan went out into the street to talk.

"They've released Mesut Mumcu. The journalist brigade made such a thing of it… but it turned out to be a false lead," he said, when he came back inside.

"What were they expecting?"

"They thought Mesut Mumcu had had Müller killed and they expected Mumcu to confess the moment he was arrested. They were just living in hope but, after all these years, they weren't going to be handed Mesut on a plate. Unfortunately, we didn't have reason enough to keep the guy inside even for a couple of nights. If he'd said, 'I had him killed', then what? What prosecutor would base a case on that?"

I was hearing this for the first time and immediately added it to my notebook of legal nuggets.

"But you think there was a love angle to this murder and the murderer was a woman."

"Even if the murderer wasn't a woman…" He was less sure about this since our conversation of the previous evening. His face had turned a purplish-red colour; he gave up trying to moderate his language just because he was in the company of a woman.

"Tell me, what hit man would think of killing someone with a hair-dryer? Come on, think about it, who would bother with that? Never mind having to take along extension leads, never mind having to find a hair-dryer… What idiot would do that? He'd pull out a gun, empty the magazine into the bastard's chest, finished, done with. And he'd go home to the arms of his lover."

I lit the first cigarette of the day. What he said was reasonable despite the way he said it.

"I'm not saying anything against anyone. Just because Müller was put inside for drugs when he was young, the lads think he was doing a bit of business. They'll pursue that line of inquiry now and make out the prick was doing business with the Mumcu brothers. I ask you, were the bastards going to get the film crew to carry white powder stuffed in their pockets?"

As well as his face going red, his eyes were now bulging. I can't bear it when people get irate and spray spittle in my face.

"Never mind all that," I said. "Let's have a drink."

"Yeah of course, let's have a drink! Have you any *rakı*?"

"I was thinking of cola or something."

"In that case, let's drink cola, my darling."

As I took the cola bottle out of the refrigerator, I could sense him standing behind me. He moved aside my hair with one hand, kissed the nape of my neck and undid the belt of my shorts. He slipped his hand deep inside my knickers. When he took his hand out, he turned my face and body towards him and, gazing into my eyes, undid the zip of his trousers. His dark, swollen penis lay against my belly as if it were a gun with which he was threatening me, as if when his gun fired, my intestines would explode.

The cola bottle was still in my hand, like a link to the real world where at any moment a crime-fiction addict might come through the door, a tourist might choose my shop as the best place to ask for directions, or a friend might turn up having left work early and tired of wandering the streets in the heat.

For all those reasons, when he tried to take the bottle from my hand, I wouldn't give it to him. There, behind the orange-green-and-blue-striped curtain that separated the kitchen from the shop, I stood with my shorts and knickers around my ankles, holding on to my cola bottle like a child clutching a toy truck as he waits to receive a scolding for having wet himself.

His penis glistened like shot silk, now purple, now wine-coloured.

He was shaking his head from side to side. "You don't want me," he said, more as a statement of fact than a question.

That was the sort of thing people say after forty years of marriage, something a woman might say to her husband before taking a sip of whisky from the glass on the bedside table and asking, "Is there somebody else?" When he said, "No way," she'd insist, "I know there's another woman, blonde and much younger than me. I've seen you with her." As he saw his wife gulp down one whisky after another, he'd realize this was the opportunity he'd been waiting for. He'd take a deep breath and say, "Yes, there is someone else. I'm in love with her." The woman, her hair dishevelled, would pour another whisky and the curtain would come down. Any female spectator would then turn angrily on her husband, while a male would set off home to his crumpled, familiar sheets with dreams of a young blonde lover.

"You don't want me," he said again. This time more distantly, not to me but to himself, as if he was trying to see himself through my eyes and work out why I didn't want him, as if it was possible to find an instant solution to this "lack of desire".

I put the bottle that I'd been holding tight to my bosom on the little table that served as a kitchen surface.

"It's a bit presumptuous to say I don't want you," I said, as if it wasn't me talking but someone else.

As I uttered this odd sentence, I realized his penis was now whitish-pink, paler than the rest of his body.

"What does presumptuous mean?" he asked, as he put it back in his trousers.

We both looked down at my shorts and knickers lying around my ankles. He fixed his eyes on my legs as if the answer to his question was written on my knees.

In my tiny kitchen, it took barely one step to reach my side. He dressed me with an intimate tenderness that only a man who felt genuine love would display.

If it had been anyone other than him, if he hadn't been a policeman, or if my strongest prejudice had not been against the police, I don't know how I would have felt. But at that moment, I just felt as though I had been punched in the stomach.

Once Batuhan had left to walk down to Karaköy, I decided the day would be pretty unsatisfactory unless I spoke to Ali Vardar. After dithering for about ten minutes, I finally left the shop at six o'clock, hoping the man would still be at his office.

I stood in front of the building in Asmalımescit Street, where I often used to meet Fofo, but the door was locked. Ali Vardar's name did not appear on any of the doorbells. I thought I must be mistaken so I went to look at some other buildings. His name was on none of them, so I returned to the first building and pressed a bell that belonged to one of the law firms there. The man who answered said that Ali Vardar had moved to another office two months ago; if the hall porter didn't have the new address, I should ring the manager's bell.

It was six thirty-five when I sank into the armchair opposite the secretary's desk in Ali Vardar's new Gümüşsuyu office. "I bet there's a wonderful view from here," I thought. The secretary had disappeared inside the office to "ask him a favour" at my insistence, because apparently Mr Vardar did not see anyone without an appointment.

With his hands in the air as if in prayer Muslim style, and wearing a busily-coloured paisley-design cravat, Ali Vardar waltzed in crying out, "Kati, what a surprise!"

"Seeing me might be something of a bad surprise, Ali," I said.

He pretended not to hear. Those men are like that; they pretend not to hear anything that disturbs them. Ali put his hand between my shoulder blades and pushed me firmly into his office. "What would you like to drink?" he asked.

When he asked this, I felt for the first time a twinge of sympathy towards this disagreeable man.

"Something strong. Have you got any whisky?"

"Of course I have. Ice?"

"Ice and soda, if you have both," I said. In this heat, I needed it.

As Ali went out to get the whisky, I asked if I could use the telephone. I had phoned Lale before leaving the shop, but her secretary had said she was in a meeting and not taking calls. I hoped the meeting was now over.

Hearing Lale's voice filled me with pleasure. I told her I needed her advice about something and would be at her place by nine o'clock at the latest. I felt better for having spoken to her.

Ali returned with two glasses. One of them was filled almost to the brim with whisky, ice and soda, the other with an orange-coloured liquid.

Unable to contain my curiosity, I asked what he was drinking.

"Campari Orange. I had it last year for the first time when I was in Italy. Do you want to try it?" He pushed the glass across the table towards me.

"Thanks, but I know it," I said.

Actually, I loved the way these new crazes caught on, like the Montgolfiers' hot-air balloons.

"I must say, it's a drink that suits your new image," I said.

"I doubt if you came here to discuss drinks with me," he retorted.

"I saw your picture in the papers this morning. That's why I came."

"Picture? What picture?" He wasn't pretending.

"It was taken with Mesut Mumcu, somewhere near Fethiye. I don't know when."

"My photo was taken? I'm so busy I never look at the papers. I'll tell the girl to get some." He picked up the phone and called his secretary on the internal line.

After putting the phone down, he said, "I don't get the connection between my picture being in the papers and your being here."

"I'm interested in a murder and Mesut Mumcu's name came up."

"What do you mean you're 'interested in a murder'?"

"My friend Petra Vogel is the star of *A Thousand and One Nights in the Harem*, which is to be filmed in Istanbul."

"Do they suspect her now?"

I fobbed him off with a fatuous argument.

"No. But she happened to witness certain events. It's aroused my curiosity and I want to find out about this murder."

"I'm not the person you need to see."

"Don't talk like that, Ali. I just want you to tell me what you know, that's all."

"The only thing I know is that Mesut Mumcu had no connection with it."

"I didn't say he had any connection with it anyway. Whoever heard of a gangland boss ordering his men to throw a hair-dryer into a bathtub to kill someone? And no hired killer would have such imagination. I don't suspect Mesut Mumcu either. What I find suspicious is that Mumcu handed such a costly project to someone as inadequate as Müller. The screenplay was written by one of the best writers of this century, yet the director was to be Müller. Don't you think there's something strange about that?"

"Who wrote the film script?"

"Giacomo Donetti."

"Ah," he said. I felt sure that, despite his holiday in Italy last summer, he had no idea who Donetti was. But we weren't competing in a general knowledge quiz.

"I think this Donetti story is a coincidence." He pronounced the name of the great Donetti in such a way that I had to bite my lip to stop myself from laughing. "I doubt if Mesut would be capable of finding a famous scriptwriter." He stopped. "He set up the production company for Yusuf, his brother-in-law, so maybe Yusuf found this writer. Or maybe the German partners engaged him. But I can assure you that Mesut had nothing to do with it."

"Fine, but your client has been investing a lot of money in the film. Why would he squander his money on Müller? Surely he must have done his research and weighed up Müller against Donetti and Petra Vogel? After all he is a businessman of sorts, and he undoubtedly wants to make money."

Ali murmured to himself, "Businessman... businessman..." I felt as if I must have been the first person ever to call a gangland boss a businessman, yet I'd had no intention of straining either Turkish definitions or the intelligence of a Turkish lawyer.

"Yes, you could call him a businessman," he said finally.

Again, I couldn't resist it.

"If you don't think the term 'businessman' is right for this man, why have you taken on his case, for God's sake?"

"He may not be a businessman, but everyone has the right to a defence," he said without hesitation.

It was a good line, but one that would only impress a dusty academic. I didn't bother to ask my second question.

"What I meant was, whether he's a businessman or not, he's in it to make money, isn't he? Like everyone else."

"I understand what you're trying to say. You're saying that, if he wanted to make money with this film, why work with someone like Müller? OK, how do you know that he didn't make money from Müller's films? Maybe his films made a lot of money."

I admit I'd made a logical mistake, which Ali had spotted straight away. In the film business, as in all businesses, there was no connection between making a profitable product and a good one.

"You're right. Fine, but why do you think they bought the film rights to Donetti's book? Surely there's something odd there at least."

"I'm sure he has something to say on the matter but, as I said, I'm not the person to talk to about these matters."

"You're right," I repeated, like the agreeable sort of person I am. I immediately moved on to my second set of questions.

"Why did the police arrest your client and why did they release him? I can at least talk to you about that, can't I?"

"Did they arrest and release him? Where did you hear he'd been released?"

I forced down the mouthful I'd just taken from my glass, trying to find a plausible reason for my knowing about Mumcu's release.

"Well, I thought he'd been released, but has he in fact?"

"Yes, he was released this afternoon, a few hours ago." Ali hadn't suspected anything. Actually, he'd never have become a lawyer if his imagination had been fertile enough to conjure up visions of me flirting with policemen.

"Why did they release him?"

"They couldn't hold on to him, that's why." He was showing his skills as a lawyer. Mesut Mumcu wasn't innocent.

"So why did they arrest him?"

"To intimidate him. They thought he'd be scared, get upset and confess. Even you thought that. Mesut would never have anyone killed with a hair-dryer. Don't the police realize that? It's nonsense whichever way you look at it."

"Why were you with him when he was arrested?"

"He sent for me. They visited his Istanbul house and office, and he thought they'd come to see me anyway. What's wrong with that? Does it mean the man's guilty?"

"No, I was just asking. Why are you getting so angry?"

"I'm not angry."

I had no wish to continue this pointless conversation, despite the whisky and ice, and the views of Topkapı Palace, Haydarpaşa and the Prince's Islands. What did the Turkish ancients say? Whenever there's a noise, it's best to leave.

Whatever that means.

I crossed the Bosphorus Bridge, which I and Istanbul taxi drivers call the "first bridge". I was listening to *La Flaca*, an album by Jarabe de Palo that Fofo gave me, and I made a resolution that for one day, or a few hours at least, I would put aside all thoughts of the murder and Batuhan. What I really wanted was to eat a proper meal, like green beans in olive oil, and have a long chat with Lale.

As I entered the house, I was greeted by a pervasive smell that made me realize my dream of a proper meal that evening was not going to happen. Lale had her sleeves rolled up and was about to embark on some Turkish creation based on an Italian recipe of pasta with garlic yoghurt.

"How did you know I'd be early?"

"I didn't. I was starving and I thought I'd leave some for you."

"I thought we'd go out for dinner," I said, almost crying. I guessed she'd bought that triple-coloured pasta, which was dancing so sadly and spiritlessly in the water, especially for tonight and she certainly wasn't prepared to throw it out.

"Don't be silly, not after all this work. Anyway I bought coloured pasta," she said, mixing the rinsed strands with yoghurt.

As we ate our pasta under the walnut tree that shaded the tiny back garden, we both fell deep into thought. I knew very well that my friend Lale couldn't bear long silences.

"How is it?" she asked, meaning the pasta. She knew full well that I wouldn't say, "Awful."

"A bit too salty," I said.

"I wish I could retrieve every grain of salt I've ever wasted," she said, more seriously than one might have expected.

"Where did that come from?"

"I've just found out. The cleaner Havva told me. Salt is sacred."

"Well, there's no chance of retrieving the salt you wasted on this pasta. It would've been better if you'd agreed to go out for dinner as I suggested," I said.

"Don't be silly. It's not that salty," she said, laughing.

"Anyway, why is salt sacred?"

"I don't know. Havva doesn't know either."

There was silence again.

"Maybe it has something to do with Lot's wife," I said, my mouth crammed full of pasta in an attempt to fill my stomach.

"What's it got to do with Lot's wife?"

"When the family was fleeing after the Sodom and Gomorrah disaster, the woman looked back and was turned to salt. Lot and his two daughters did what they were told and didn't look back. Out of that enormous tribe, they were the only three to be saved," I said.

"I thought Lot's wife was turned to stone."

"No, I'm sure it was salt." Lale knew very well that I could compete with anyone on Old Testament stories, so I thought she wouldn't continue with this argument. However, she did.

"Salt or stone, whichever it was, it was all because she wanted to see their property, which had burned to the ground in Sodom and Gomorrah. She looked at the city one last time because she couldn't bear to lose everything, isn't that right? I think —"

"No, she wasn't looking at their property. Where did you get that from?"

"Of course she was. She was looking back at their property for one last time, otherwise why look back?"

"Look, it's a dreadful, sexist, anti-female..."

As always when I was exasperated, emphatic Turkish words eluded me. I gave up trying to find the best word and continued.

"Of course it's always women who are after money and property. Of course it's greedy women who grieve over burning property. It's they who turn round and look, they who turn to salt. Whereas Lot wasn't bothered about property at all. He had no strong interest in money, valuables or property, because he was a man. Lot kept looking straight ahead. Naturally, that night in the cave, his daughters got him drunk and became pregnant by him. Lot was so drunk he didn't know he'd slept with his daughters, yet he wasn't so drunk that he couldn't get an erection." I was shouting the second part of the Sodom and Gomorrah story about how daughters would get their fathers drunk and sleep with them in order to propagate the family line.

"Calm down, please," said Lale. "So what if women are greedy? So what if Lot's wife turned and looked at their burning property?"

"What if the woman wanted one last look at the city she loved? Don't you see the difference, Lale? Surely there's a difference between a greedy, avaricious woman and a woman who loves the hills and open spaces of the city where she lives, her house and garden, the honeysuckle by her front door?"

"Of course there is, but what difference does it make if Lot's wife looked back? Is that what we're arguing about?"

"This has nothing to do with Lot's wife," I said. "It's one of many things people say against women, as if it's in their biological make-up. People say women care about valuables and property as if it were a scientific fact, like menstruation or childbirth."

"Salt…"

"Stop talking about salt. There are certain anti-female prejudices and clichés. You know that better than me. Indeed you've said yourself that people ask if you find it tiring being publishing director of a large newspaper. Would they worry so much about you getting tired if you were a man, I wonder? I tell you, they wouldn't. Why do they care so much about you getting tired? If you stayed at home raising your kids like other women, you wouldn't get tired, would you? Women should do light work designed for women, shouldn't they?" I'd gone too far this time, and I doubted that my example about Lale had anything to do with what we'd been discussing. However, at that moment I was in no state to put forward a sensible and coherent argument.

"You're upset, darling," said Lale. She was maintaining that special cool-headedness that businesswomen have and refusing to engage in a war of words with me. I thought she should be proud of herself for that. In fact, it's the quality that separates me and my sort from her and her sort.

Lale gathered up the plates and went inside. I sat lethargically on my own in the garden for a while and then followed her into the kitchen.

"What happened today?" she asked. She was putting the dirty dishes into the dishwasher.

"I've been trying to count the stars, yet I don't even know how many teeth I have in my mouth. But hey, so what?" I said.

"That's a really nice saying. Did you translate it from German?" she said. Lale never admits that my Turkish is any good; she's always trying to catch me making a mistake.

"I don't know. My father used to say it. It means you haven't a clue."

"Not having a clue, what does that have to do with anything, sweetie? You started doing this detective business as a hobby. Is there anything at stake here? No. If you don't uncover the facts of this murder, so what?"

"What hobby? You talk as if all I've done is look at a few toy guns this week. Someone has died and a murderer is still at large out there. You call this a hobby?"

"I may have used the wrong word. What I meant to say was that this isn't your job. You're not a policeman or

125

anything, are you? You're a woman who sells books in your own special way."

"Let's change the subject. I realize you're just trying to calm me down but, believe me, there's no point. Anyway, my problem has nothing to do with my so-called hobby."

"Then what is it to do with? Have you found yourself surrounded by sexist men?" I knew for sure that, as the evening wore on, the things I'd said in our argument earlier that evening would be used against me.

"You know as well as I do that what I said was true. They twist everything at women." I lit one of the cigarettes that lay on the kitchen worktop and added, "If not everything, a lot of things."

"I'll give you a column in our newspaper if you like. Your Turkish is bad enough. You wouldn't stand out as a foreigner among the other columnists. What's more, you're an infidel."

"Why is my Turkish so bad?" I said, feeling irritated.

"You don't 'twist something at', you 'twist something against'," she said, as if she was the first girl to learn how to read and write.

"If you spoke German as well as my Turkish… Well, not German, because that's a difficult language. But if you learn to speak any language as well as I speak Turkish, I'll kiss your forehead in admiration."

"Did you come to quarrel with me, Kati? If that's really why you came, you didn't pick a good time. I'm too tired to fight and anyway the English I know is sufficient for me."

How come I'd resorted to competing with my best friend in this stupid way? "OK, fine, you're right," I said, and immediately offered to make coffee to show there were no hard feelings.

126

"I can't drink coffee in the evenings any more. I'll have a weak tea. You don't need to brew it, there are tea bags in there," she said.

I'm five years older than Lale, so if coffee stops her sleeping, think what it must do to me. I made myself some mint tea.

We sipped our tea in the living room on the middle floor of the house, and I told Lale what had happened with Batuhan.

"If you want to sleep with a man, then go ahead of course. Does Germany have an ethical rule that says you can't sleep with a policeman?" she said. Lale was still playing masterfully with my nerves.

"What's it got to do with Germany? My dislike of policemen runs much deeper than I'd realized. I didn't know I felt so strongly about them."

"Ah, that's why you're so against prejudices and clichés."

Remorselessly, she continued to rake over what I'd said at dinner; she was going to carry on probing until I caved in and apologized for everything I'd ever said and ever would say.

"Can't we have a bit of a break?" I asked.

"I'm trying to understand why you were shouting."

"There's nothing to understand. I'm upset. You said it yourself."

"Are you upset because of Batuhan?"

"I'm upset because I don't know what to do. In normal conditions, I'd want to be with a man, but because he's a policeman…"

"I don't know why you've made such a problem out of this. Do you want to be with him, or not? What have normal conditions or abnormal conditions got to do with it?"

"OK, but why don't I want to be with this man? Is the world awash with men who are good-looking, charming police-academy graduates?"

"Am I missing something here?" She suddenly narrowed her eyes and shook her head from side to side as if she'd made a big discovery. "Now I understand. You want my permission to be with this man. If I say, 'What a nice man,' it'll put your mind at ease," she said.

"Of course it would put me at ease, but I've been with men before without your approval."

"But this time it's different. Use your head: it's not just your prejudice. You're thinking of the people around you. What would Fofo say? What would Pelin say? What would çaycı Recai think? You've become a real Turk! You're a Turk through and through!" This discovery amused Lale greatly. Laughing, she continued her monologue.

"What would your neighbours say, eh? If anyone saw him going in and out of your apartment in police uniform… What would everyone think? OK, I'll tell you what everyone would think. They'd think that Kati has found herself a policeman. I don't think anyone will stop talking to you because of this, darling. And it isn't as if he's a traffic cop; he's a policeman who works on homicides."

"Inspector," I pointed out. "And he doesn't wear uniform." In fact, he looked better in uniform than in plain clothes, but it didn't matter. "And if he was a traffic cop, so what?"

"Well, this is what comes of refusing to read the papers. You don't know the results of a public-opinion research project that has rocked Turkey. Apparently, the professional group with the most cases of bribery turned out to be traffic police."

128

"They found that every fifth person has bribed a traffic policeman," I said, finishing Lale's statement. Even if I didn't read the papers, I knew everything and never missed an opportunity of demonstrating it. Lale again collapsed into peals of laughter. Ignoring her, I continued talking.

"But Lale darling, I don't remember that research rocking Turkey."

Between her bouts of laughter, Lale was crying out, "Wonderful, wonderful!" just as she did whenever we met her grandmother.

"What is it? Tell me, then we can both laugh," I said.

"What do you mean 'every fifth person'? Speak properly. You translated that from German, didn't you? Where do you find these things? 'Every fifth person.' Speak properly. Did you or didn't you translate that?"

"Well how do you say it?" I said, instantly realizing that the Turkish should have been 'one in five people'. "Yes, I translated it. So what? Turks translate lots of things from English. For instance, did the expression 'Take care' always exist in Turkish? I translate from German, not English. Anyway, I'm bored with your attitude; you sound like a headmistress, psychiatrist or Chairman of the Turkish Language Association," I said. She could tease me about anything, apart from my Turkish!

I went downstairs to look for my bag and car keys, and Lale came running after me like a naughty child.

Regret is futile, and broken hearts are not mended with a couple of sweet words.

I found a parking space right in front of the door to my apartment block. I had slept until midday so I wasn't feeling the least bit tired, but my head was swimming from the smell of garlic I was exuding and from the bickering with Lale. All I wanted was to drink gallons of water, brush my teeth and take a warm shower.

The moment I opened my apartment door, I sensed something odd had happened. It was my habit to double-lock the door, but that night the door opened after one turn of the key.

"I obviously forgot to double-lock when I went out this morning. It must have been because of the migraine," I mused, and thought no more of it.

I took off my sandals in the entrance hall and walked barefoot on the cold stone floor to the kitchen where I drank a large glass of water. In Istanbul we have to buy bottled drinking water because Istanbul tap water contains enough bacteria and microbes to kill an ox. I can't complain about having to carry water from the corner shop to my apartment because the shop boy does that, but I really miss turning on the tap for a glass of water.

Without going into the front room, I headed straight for the rear part of the apartment, where my bedroom and Fofo's, the bathroom and my study were. I undressed in front of the bathroom mirror and got into the shower.

Regretting that I'd thrown my favourite pink shorts and Donald Duck T-shirt into the laundry basket that morning, I put on a flowered dress and covered my shoulders with a towel to absorb the drips from my hair.

I then went into the front living room to watch television. If, instead of going into the living room, I'd gone straight to my bedroom, counted a few sheep and gone to sleep, the poor man wouldn't have woken me up. He would have simply left and that meeting would never have happened. However, I went into the living room.

The bright light from the entrance hall made the living room seem dark and I didn't see the man sitting in the armchair. People usually only see what they expect to see. However, when I turned on the lamp that stood on the table between the sofa and the armchair, I couldn't help but see him. He was right in front of my nose.

"I wonder if he'll disappear if I close my eyes?" I admit that was the thought that seized me, despite it resembling a line out of fiction. But the fact that Mesut Mumcu was waiting for me in my living room was as absurd as fiction.

He was sitting in my armchair, looking much more impressive than his photograph in that morning's newspaper. He was both impressive and smartly dressed. He wore a linen suit in the colour they call Turkish-Parliament blue, a mauve shirt and black moccasins. He had short black hair, large thick lips and a self-confidence born of his ability to create fearful respect in those around him. I have to admit that until ten years ago, men like him, whose ego and presence filled the room, were immensely attractive to me. However, in recent years, as the wrinkles around the eyes have increased, I've begun to seek out different qualities in men; perhaps it's the wisdom of age or something. I'm sure that you, my dear readers, know what I mean.

Apparently worried that I'd cry out in fear, Mesut Mumcu took the trouble to stand up, point towards the sofa and say, "Do sit down." I wasn't really used to anyone showing me hospitality in my own home and in my confusion I came out with a stupid remark.

"So, it was first come, first served for the armchair this evening," I said. I pulled away the towel that I'd put over my shoulders to catch the drips from my hair and spread it over the arm of the sofa. I was trying to maintain at least a little composure, despite my hair looking as though it had been licked by a cat. Mesut studied me hard, starting with my shoulders, dwelling at length on my bra-less breasts, and roaming down to my bordeaux-coloured toenails. Finally, he leaned his head to one side, indicating his pleasure and approval of what he saw.

I had recently read an article saying that in the Muslim world the home is considered a sacred place and is untouchable. For instance in Iran, the Revolutionary Guards would only attack a house if they were sure someone had been murdered in there, which meant everyone could drink alcohol and fornicate at home. Clearly Mesut Mumcu knew nothing about this culture of the home being sacred in the Muslim world. He was probably also unaware that he would have to sweep up the salt he had wasted.

"How did you open the door?" I asked.

"The boys opened it," he said. He wasn't the sort to let such minor details bother him. But I'd sensed that before he'd said anything.

I even wondered if Mumcu's boys had kept the parking space in front of the apartment free for me.

"We couldn't find an ashtray," he said.

It was clearly intended as a favour to me that, having been unable to find an ashtray, they had not smoked. They might have smoked and stubbed out their cigarette butts on my beautiful Hereke carpet. However, my problem now was about there being a second person in the apartment rather than about my carpet. It meant someone else was somewhere in the darkness of the other half of the sitting room.

Determined to keep calm at all costs, I said, "There's an ashtray next to the sink in the kitchen." I spoke in a voice that could be heard at the other end of the room.

Nobody moved.

I'd had enough and wasn't prepared to put up with any more. "I'm going to have a whisky. Would you like one?" I asked, again in a loud voice.

"With ice," said Mesut Mumcu. The other person didn't make a sound.

When I returned from the kitchen with the whiskies, two iced and one with ice and soda, and an ashtray, Mesut Mumcu was comfortably settled in my armchair with his legs crossed. The other man or woman, whoever it was, was still nowhere to be seen.

"It was you on the telephone yesterday, wasn't it?" he said.

"Yes," I replied. He was referring to my call from Petra's room.

"I understand you saw Ali today." He meant Fofo's former lover.

"Yeah," I said.

"And I understand you spoke to a fellow from the tribe yesterday."

"Who? Who did I speak to?" This time I really didn't understand.

"From our tribe. What's his name? He works for a newspaper."

He meant the crime reporter I saw the previous day.

"Now I know who you mean. Yes, I met him," I said. I remembered how he had written my name and telephone number on the back of a cigarette packet.

Before drinking his whisky, he lifted up his glass saying, "May our worst days be like this."

"Not mine," I said. Apart from finding the parking space in front of the door, nothing very good had happened to me that day. I wondered whether I should tell the other person to come and get his whisky, but decided against it. He would if he wanted to.

Mesut was offended, being the sensitive person he was.

"It was very unseemly for us to enter your home like this. You're a guest in our country and what we did is unacceptable. We feel ashamed about that. But we can't turn up in the daytime and ring the bell, nor can we come to the bookshop to buy a book. Everyone would laugh at us. And, don't get me wrong, it wouldn't be good for you either. This was the best way."

He could have been right. It would probably not have been good for me to have been seen consorting with a gangland boss so soon after a policeman. Anyway, it was unlikely they'd read my diary while they were waiting since, to save money, they had just sat there in the dark without even switching on the lights.

"OK, we'll suppose this was the best way of seeing me, but why do you need to see me?" I said, without giving any clue that I was a strong woman who was used to danger.

"Why are you getting mixed up in this business?"

"Which business?"

"This murder business."

"To find the murderer, that's why."

"Finding murderers is police business. All this isn't right for you. You could find yourself the target of some stray bullet, anything might happen. Don't get me wrong. We've clinked glasses together. Nothing will happen to you because of us. I swear to God that we'd never lay a finger on a woman, but you never know what will happen in this world."

"So, do you think someone from 'this world' is behind the murder? Or was Müller killed to settle some score?" I'd taken courage from what he said and started throwing a series of questions at him.

"Who it was and why it happened, we don't know either. It might have been one of our enemies, it might have been someone trying to muscle in on our patch. We have a lot of enemies in this world. Many didn't want us released and would like us back inside. It could've been anyone. We won't have any peace until the murderer is found," he said. He'd become nervous and he put his right hand in his pocket to pull out some amber worry beads.

"You mean until the police find the murderer," I said. Either he did not understand, or he ignored what I said. He continued to twiddle his worry beads with agile fingers.

"We're looking for the murderer as well. Whoever it is, he certainly didn't kill the man as a favour to us. Look, who do the police think of first? Us. Has anyone thought why we would want to kill the director of a film that we'd invested in? Are we such idiots that we'd bring the man here from Germany and then kill him? Have our arms shrunk or something? What do they think we are? We'd have killed him in Germany, wouldn't we?"

That was one point of view of course.

"Why did you go into this film business?" I asked, ignoring, or trying to ignore, all this talk about killing and having people killed.

"We went into it because my sister Yakut's husband wanted it, and we said he could look after it." So we'd finally got round to the brother-in-law Yusuf, who had been mentioned so often over the last few days. But first, there was something else I needed to sort out.

"When you say 'we', who do you mean?" I asked. I was ready to enjoy some sort of cat-and-mouse game trying to get this out of him.

"Us?"

"Well, you keep on saying things like, 'We said he could look after it'. Who do you mean by 'we'?" I kept my eyes fixed on the darkness.

However, Mesut waved his hand at his chest and said, "Well... us."

"Hah!" I said. He was using the plural whenever he referred to himself. While referring to me as *sen*, meaning "thou", he referred to himself as "we". It was a good way for a feudal lord to put a distance between himself and his villagers.

I poured the other whisky I'd prepared into my glass, spilling half of it on the coffee table, took a large sip and reminded him where we'd got to so that he would continue speaking.

"You said you went into this business for Yakut's husband," I said, going straight to the point. I wasn't going to stand on ceremony with him any more.

"Yakut's husband!?..." He frowned for a moment as if trying to remember the man's name. "Hah! Yusuf! Yusuf! Yakut's husband became a Muslim and took the name Yusuf. His real name is German."

136

When he uttered the word German, he remembered that I too was German. He scrutinized me from top to toe again.

"You're German, but you speak Turkish so well," he said. I admit I was gradually beginning to like Mesut.

"Our Yusuf hasn't managed to learn it. In fact, he and Yakut always speak German at home. We keep telling her, 'Let the man learn Turkish'. But no. Our sister has good German and French. Our older brother Maksut, bless him, he's a progressive type. He said, 'I'm going to educate this girl.' Nothing wrong with that, is there?"

"It's more important for girls to study," I said. That's what my hairdresser's sixteen-year-old apprentice always says when I go for a blow-dry. He takes pride in working so that his sister can go to school.

"Of course, it's more important," he agreed. "Men do the hard work and earn the bread, so what are the girls to do? Are they supposed to become… excuse me, but are they supposed to become whores?"

After all those years, I now understood what my hairdresser's apprentice meant when he said, "Miss, it's more important for girls to go to school." What strange ideas these Turks and Kurds have.

"We have property. Our brothers aren't dependent on anyone. But you never know what God has in store. You must look to the future and never rely on the past," he said.

"Yusuf…" I said again, wanting to return to the main subject. There'd been enough coffee-house philosophy.

"Yusuf?" he asked in surprise, obviously thinking we'd finished with that subject. Wasn't it possible to talk to someone about the same thing for even ten minutes? He remembered where we'd got to and continued.

137

"Yusuf had business dealings in Germany. When he came here… Well, he couldn't learn the language, so what could the kid do? We didn't want him working with Yakut. You can't have a man working alongside his wife. That wouldn't do at all. So, we offered to do some business with the Germans. Of course it had to be something suitable for Yusuf. The kid plays the piano and so on, did you know that? He's interested in the arts. It was he who suggested this film-production business, and we accepted. If only we'd known what was going to happen!" He shook his head in disgust. "Disasters appear where you least expect them."

"I don't know if you've noticed, but there's something strange about this business," I said. "The writer of the book you had made into a script is very famous. The book's constantly on the best-seller list; it's very widely read and has been translated into over thirty languages. However, your director… I mean your former director, Kurt Müller, is a fourth-rate cinema man with no decent film to his name; he was just a good businessman. That bothered me right from the start. Why was Kurt Müller chosen to be the director?"

"That's how it was. He was very famous. Ali, our lawyer, said so. You must know that too because we spoke to Ali this evening. We'd asked Yusuf about Müller, but didn't get involved after that. Yusuf went to and from Germany setting up all the agreements. We have too much work and not enough time. We can't do everything, so we left it to Yusuf. We had nothing to do with it."

"OK, but what did Yusuf say? Why that film script and that director?"

138

"It was because of that Italian guy that we went into this business. The German production company had bought the film and was looking for a Turkish partner."

"Do you mean they bought the film rights to the book?" I asked.

"Yes, yes. Something like that. Yusuf thought it would be a good start for our company. That director wasn't yet on the scene. We don't really know anything about it; you should talk to Yusuf," he said. Then he leaned his head over his left shoulder and turned to the right as if wondering why he was saying all this.

"Hey, I've forgotten how we got onto this."

I'd noticed before that when people, especially men, started talking to me, they'd open up and say more than they should, all sorts of things they shouldn't say. But this time, I'd surpassed myself. Every man who set foot in my sitting room seemed to end up singing like a nightingale.

"Forget about Yusuf and who the murderer is. That kind of thing isn't for you. You look after your own business. If anything bad happened to you, we wouldn't like it either," he said, frowning.

He rose and held out his hand.

"Thank you for the whisky. Sorry for disturbing you. Don't hesitate to call if you need anything." He took a visiting card from his pocket and pressed it into my hand. I didn't know that gangland bosses had visiting cards.

"Write my mobile number down," he said. "It's my private number. Only two or three colleagues have it." He took a chunky black Mont Blanc fountain pen from his jacket pocket and handed it to me.

As Mesut Mumcu moved towards the door to leave, I said, "I want to meet Yusuf."

He turned towards me with one eyebrow raised.

"Yeah, of course you can meet him. But I don't know what Yakut would say." We were standing opposite each other in the entrance hall where the light lit up his whole face. He scrutinized me with a carnal gaze and a half-smile that did not detract from his seriousness.

I drew back slightly and covered my mouth with my hand so that he would not smell the garlic on my breath. "I'm serious," I said.

He shrugged his shoulders. "So are we," he said. "Come to our beach house in the morning and we'll talk there. You'll see Yusuf, and we'll see you."

As he turned towards the stairs, I whispered behind him, "What time? Where's your beach house? How will I find it?"

"We'll send the boys to fetch you. Nothing to worry about. Don't worry, my darling," he said finally, and disappeared down the stairs.

After Mesut Mumcu had left, I didn't even attempt to go to bed. I wouldn't have been able to sleep anyway. I watched the ice melting in the glass and downed another glass of whisky. Even if I couldn't find the murderer, nobody could say I'd been wasting my time after the mass of admiration I had received over the last week from the police and *mafiosi*. Instead of being greeted by cats rubbing around my legs, like most single women living in Cihangir, I had gangland bosses waiting for me in my sitting room. In that respect, my situation was definitely better than theirs. Given the choice, which woman would prefer a cat to a man? Of course, I mean a choice in the real sense, not the choice between a pale, hairless, male German ecologist and a cat.

Despite the pink sleeping pill, I only managed to go to sleep as dawn was breaking.

I was woken up by the doorbell.

Opening one eye, I saw that the clock by my bed showed ten fifty. Whoever was at the door had stuck his finger on my bell and was making it ring continuously. Summoning all my willpower, I managed to get my body out of bed. I made my way towards the door and leaned out of the sitting-room window to see who it was. It was a man I didn't know.

"Who do you want?" I called out.

"Miss Kati," he said.

"That's me," I said.

"Mr Mumcu sent me to fetch you. He's waiting," he said.

"Wonderful," I thought, as if I had planned to get up early to get ready. Once again, I'd turned off the alarm in the hope of sleeping late.

"Will you wait a moment? I'm just coming," I called out, and without wasting any more time ran straight to my bedroom. Running about inside the apartment saves quite a lot of time. After all, my apartment is about four times the size of one in Germany.

It took me ten minutes to decide what to wear, and at least the same to do my make-up. By the time I was finally ready and downstairs, I thought the man would have tired of waiting and left, but I was wrong. The driver must have passed a severe tolerance test as a result of hanging around outside hair salons for the women in Mesut's life, because he didn't seem at all perturbed at having to wait twenty minutes in the middle of the street. With a politeness that was at odds with his large frame and his face, scarred from left cheek to eyebrow, he opened the rear door of the brand-new Jaguar that was standing in front of my apartment building and invited me to get in.

Inside the car, a device, which was clearly expensive judging from the volume of its sound, was thumping out a folk song:

> *Think once more, think again,*
> *Is there no end to this pain?*
> *Woh wo woh woh,*
> *Woh wo woh woh,*
> *Let me look into your eyes,*
> *Do I see love, do I see lies,*
> *Let me tell you, yes or no.*

Before switching on the engine, he shouted to make himself heard, "Do you mind the music, miss?"

"Perhaps you could turn it down a little," I shouted back.

There was no further conversation. We passed some guards standing in front of the awesome outer gate of a villa in Yeniköy and drew to a halt in the garden. I jumped out without waiting for the driver to open the door. A woman was standing on the steps leading up to the house. She was wearing a maid's uniform of white miniskirt and white blouse. Seeing me alight from the car, she hopped down the steps towards me like a little bird, speaking in Turkish with an almost incomprehensibly thick accent. "Welcome Miss Kati, Mr Mumcu is waiting for you," she said.

142

Apart from her accent, it was crystal clear that she had come from some remote corner of Russia or the Balkans to work in Istanbul. However, her Turkish was not so much like that of a Slav but more like... I couldn't work out what it reminded me of.

"Where is Mr Mumcu?"

"Please," she said, indicating the door at the top of the steps.

As I ascended the marble steps behind the woman, I looked around carefully. A man was standing guard at each corner of the garden, thus making the security hut by the front door superfluous. I wondered if the nearby house where former Prime Minister Tansu Çiller lived was as tightly guarded as this.

As we went through the front door, the woman raised her right hand and said, "This way, madam, please."

I thought she must have memorized the five or six words of Turkish needed to show people around. A person capable of constructing a sentence in any language would never speak with such a strange accent. I put aside the questions that preyed on my mind about which language she used to communicate with Mesut and his men, and followed her.

The sitting room we entered made my apartment, whose size usually made me feel so proud, seem like the kitchen of a tiny shack. I couldn't help but exclaim, "Wow!"

"Extraordinary, isn't it?" said the woman.

It was interesting that someone who had memorized half a dozen words should have the word "extraordinary" in their vocabulary.

"It really is extraordinary. You're living in paradise here. Gazing out at the Bosphorus like this adds years to your life. And the longer you live here the happier you must be," I said as quickly as possible. My reason for making these fatuous remarks was to check whether or not the woman understood me.

"I've been here for two years, ma'am," she said, clearly understanding every word I said.

"Two years here, but you'd been in Turkey before that, hadn't you?" I asked. The way I'd phrased that last sentence couldn't have been understood by someone with only two years of Turkish.

"No, no. I came from Bulgaria and this is my first job here."

"OK, but where did you learn Turkish?" I asked in amazement, and with some envy.

"I speak Turkish with the other people who work here. You just pick it up after a while," she said, as if it was the most normal thing in the world to learn a language by ear. "But Turkish is really difficult," she was polite enough to add.

I realized that the few words the woman had said were not spoken with a Slavic accent, but with the accent of the Kurds who had taught her Turkish. My friend Mithat, who is from Hakkâri, says that the strongest regional accents are found among Kurds living in cities with large numbers of local Turks, such as Diyarbakir, where they learn Turkish in the street as children. On the other hand, Hakkâri Kurds learn to speak Turkish without any accent because they go to regional schools attended by the children of middle-class Turkish civil servants who are posted to the area. Clearly, most of the Kurds in the house came from Diyarbakir or its surrounding areas.

"Sit down, and I'll let Mr Mumcu know," said the woman. I asked if I could wait on the veranda, before she moved away with surprising agility.

I was gazing at the opposite shore when Mesut entered, wearing a white bathrobe. "Well, this is an honour indeed," he cried. He lit a cigar and we shook hands.

"We'll just get dressed and be right back. We always have a dip in the pool as soon as we get up, winter or summer, whatever the weather. That is of course if we're not in jail." He laughed loudly. I laughed heartily too. In this world, one could never be sure what would happen or why.

"Have you had breakfast?" I shook my head indicating "no". "Good, we'll have it together. We'll tell them to prepare it. But we'll be in the sun here, so we'll have it round the other side."

He moved away and gave orders to the two men who shadowed him everywhere. Clearly Mesut and I had the same life rhythm. We both got up towards midday.

The moment that thought passed through my mind, I jumped up from my seat. The shop? What about the shop? I'd forgotten to telephone Pelin. With some difficulty, I pushed back the iron chair and started to make my way into the sitting room, when a large well-built man appeared from nowhere and blocked my path.

"Yes, madam?"

"I... I want to make a telephone call... Or I did want to..." I said in confusion. I realized that I had been under surveillance.

"Please sit down, I'll bring a telephone to you, madam," he said.

145

I turned back and sat down. There was a strange contradiction between these burly henchmen and the smart, tastefully furnished house with its servants and antiques. Of course, Mesut himself was a man of contradictions, but this was excessive. I wondered whether Mesut had ordered the henchman to keep me under observation. People didn't seem to act on their own initiative very much in this world. If not directly by Mesut, he'd obviously been ordered to keep an eye on me by someone of authority. What were they thinking? Did they think I'd make off with the family silver?

Barely a moment had passed before the blond henchman was standing to attention next to me with a cordless telephone in his hand.

"You may go," I said.

"Make your call," he said.

With the bodyguard standing over me, I called Pelin. I confess it did occur to me to have a long conversation with my friend Cindy in Australia, as some sort of revenge. Why did this man insist on standing right next to me?

When Mesut appeared in the doorway that opened from the sitting room onto the veranda, standing in his beige linen trousers and fuchsia-and-white-striped shirt, I heaved a sigh of relief that I would be saved from the bodyguard at my side. If anyone had said twenty-four hours ago that I would feel relief at seeing Mesut in front of me, I would have said, "You're out of your mind." Life is certainly full of surprises.

"Let's go round the other side," he said, guiding me with one hand round my waist.

"Yusuf is coming too, we've sent for him. You can ask him everything you want to know," he said. The way he spoke suggested that he was used to meeting a woman's every demand, and not just demands for fur coats. As he spoke, his hand slipped a bit below my waist.

"But first, promise me that you won't put yourself in any danger," he added.

"Promise," I said, happily. "I won't put myself in any danger." Even my mother had never showed this much interest in my welfare.

When Yusuf arrived, we were wiping our mouths with starched table napkins, having finished our breakfast accompanied by four bodyguards who, with their backs towards us, appeared to be gazing continually at some distant spot on the horizon. We bowed to each other like people from the Far East. Yusuf, speaking in English, asked Mesut how he was. Mesut made a hand movement indicating that he had no time for such niceties and gestured towards me.

"My dear friend Kati" – he said in English. These Turks and Kurds, that is all those who lived in Turkey, moved very quickly to calling people "my dear" – "would like to ask you a few questions about films." He stood up as he said this, slid his hand down my back then disappeared with his four faithful henchmen.

Yusuf and I sat for a while eyeing each other at the table that was still covered with breakfast remains and half-empty plates.

"So, you're German, yes? There are loads of Germans living in Turkey. Like the pensioners in Alanya and so on... There's over fifty thousand of us. Not as many as in Mallorca, but still a lot." He popped a piece of white cheese into his mouth.

"Why are you interested in our film?" he asked, still chewing the cheese. Don't people learn as children not to speak with their mouths full, for God's sake? It wasn't a pretty sight.

"Not the film, I'm interested in the murder," I said.

"In that case, why are you interested in the murder? I presume you don't mind my asking."

Everyone I met asked me this question and I had still not found a satisfactory answer. I gave him the same sort of fatuous reply that I'd given before.

"My friend Petra Vogel was somehow involved in the murder. At least, she wasn't exactly involved, but she has been affected by it. We all want to find the murderer as soon as possible of course."

"Yes, of course. See what's happened to my brother-in-law here, and for no good reason at all. All because of me." Somehow I think this man had other problems apart from not being able to learn Turkish.

"Why did you go into the film business?"

"I liked the idea, that's why. Anyway, I had to do something eventually. I'm a bit young to retire."

"That isn't what I asked. Anyway, why this film in particular?"

"Our German partners, Phoenix Film Productions, bought the film rights to Donetti's book shortly after it was published. The production company was doing well at that time. By the time I was put in touch with them by a friend, the company's finances were not too good. For them, this was a recovery project, while for us it was our first real step into the market. We had enough money to make this film and they had the experience to put together a good production. Not a bad combination, don't you think?"

"Right from the start, I've been bothered as to why you had such high hopes... And since it was a debut for you, and a lifeline for your partner... Why a man like Kurt Müller?"

"Kurt Müller's name wasn't mentioned at first. As I said, we had the book, scriptwriter and screenplay. Our partner Mr Franz insisted on Miss Vogel taking the leading role. I could have thought of someone more suitable, but..." He didn't complete his sentence.

"Who? Türkân Şoray for example?" I said teasingly.

"Why not? You've read the book haven't you?" He raised his hand and waved it. The blond henchman who had previously attached himself to me suddenly reappeared.

"Coffee," said Yusuf, and the blond henchman disappeared. I was feeling acutely uncomfortable.

"I haven't read the book, but I know what it's about. It's the story of a female slave who is brought from Venice and who rises to the position of sultana at the Ottoman court... The book deals with the period when the woman was middle-aged, if I'm not mistaken," I said.

"You aren't mistaken. And when you thought of a middle-aged sultana, you thought of Türkân Şoray."

"Actually, Türkân Şoray would have made an overripe sultana rather than a middle-aged one," I said. I had no objection at all to the dewy-eyed, quivering-lipped stars of Turkish cinema who are nicknamed "sultana" but, painful as it might be, one of my duties as a German was to speak the truth.

"Or, if not Türkân Şoray, then perhaps Gülşen Bubikoğlu."

He pronounced the poor woman's name very badly but it seemed he knew something about female Turkish film stars.

"But Petra Vogel and the role of sultana..." He screwed up his face and continued. "If you haven't read the book, you won't know. The person in question is Sultana Handan, favourite concubine of Mehmed III and mother of Ahmed I. Sultana Handan is unknown by many historians, but Donetti claims she was Venetian, like Mehmed III's mother, Sultana Safiye. Much of the work deals with the quarrels between Handan and Safiye and court intrigues. When Handan's son is crowned Sultan Ahmed I at the age of fourteen, control of the palace falls into her hands and she wastes no time in sending Sultana Safiye to the Old Palace, along with most of her harem entourage. However, Handan is unable to enjoy her new role for long because her son dies two years after ascending to the throne. Handan's life is a tragedy, because when Safiye's son is crowned Mehmed III at the age of nineteen, he proves to be a cold-hearted murderer, despite being one of the best-educated sultans who ever lived. Handan finds herself embroiled in a struggle with both Sultana Safiye and Sultan Mehmed III. And just when the spectator thinks she has succeeded, she dies." The word "spectator" irritated me. Yusuf had really got caught up in this film business. And he knew his subject. He continued the story with enthusiasm.

"Yes, Sultana Handan wasn't an eastern woman, but she knew all about court intrigues... You've heard of the term 'Byzantine intrigue'. Historians believe the Ottoman court adopted those very same Byzantine intrigues. They behaved in exactly the same way as the Byzantines, or whatever you want to call them – Byzantines, Romans, Mediterraneans, choose what you will. But Handan was obviously not German, and it's not

a world that a German can bring to life or get inside."
Then, as if that was the culmination of what he had to
say, he stated, "I was therefore never in favour of Miss
Vogel for this part. It was Franz who insisted."

"Just a minute, who's Franz?" I asked.

"Our partner. He's the boss of Phoenix Film
Productions."

"Pardon? So many names get bandied around that I
have difficulty remembering them all."

"An oriental female actor, that is a Turk... Although
if you ask me, Turks are more Mediterranean than
eastern... Anyway, a Turk in this role would be too
oriental. Our Sultana Handan was originally Venetian,
so she shouldn't behave like a real oriental. Do you
understand what I'm saying?"

"There could be some logic in that," I said. "If the
woman in the film was not supposed to behave as if she
was in her own natural environment... I haven't read the
book, but I accept what you say." Still, imagining Petra
as a sultana was even more difficult than imagining that
the wrinkles round my eyes would disappear by the time
I woke up in the morning.

A young uniformed maid came in with two cups of
Turkish coffee and a glass of water for each of us. As she
placed the coffees on the table, I remarked, "You didn't
ask how I take my coffee." What a disgrace!

"They told me you wanted it medium sweet, ma'am. I
can make you another one straight away."

"Yes, do that. I drink it without sugar, none at all,"
I said, like a sultana in an oriental environment. The
maid hurried away with the coffee.

"How many years have you been in Turkey?" asked
Yusuf.

"Quite a while. About thirteen years."

"You seem to have resolved the problem of Turkish."

"One learns over time," I said, as if it was of no importance to me. His jealous look suggested that he was just as sensitive as I was over the matter of speaking Turkish. He resumed what he had been saying.

"Mr Franz insisted on Petra Vogel, saying she was the only person who could take on this role. I didn't argue. I had no professional experience – this was to be my first film." He leaned his chin on his clenched fist.

"The first, but not the last," I said. "I'm sure you'll find a director and continue filming. Or perhaps it would be more accurate to say you'll start filming." I was starting to feel more pity for the poor man than when I heard he'd been circumcised as a grown man in order to become a Muslim.

"We've already spent much more money than we intended. The permits arrived late; we need special permits to film in Topkapı Palace and the harem quarters. It's all taken much longer than we expected… The sets and costumes… They all cost an awful lot. The hotel expenses alone have been a big item. Many of the people working on the film have been brought from Germany; not even the lighting man is local. And then, we were going to participate in international competitions, but because of this murder it won't be ready in time…" He uttered this last sentence as if the problem was a pimple on the nose of the leading lady.

I had enough problems of my own, so I interrupted him impatiently.

"Can we get back to my question? OK, so Mr Franz insisted on Petra taking the leading role, but what did Kurt Müller have to do with all this?"

This time, my coffee was brought to me by the Bulgarian maid who had learned Diyarbakir Turkish by ear. I smiled and thanked her.

"According to what Franz told me, it was Miss Vogel who suggested Müller. She'd said they'd work well together. There may have been a bit of negotiating. Franz didn't object to Müller because his assistant director Miss Bauer was a young but very competent person. As far as I'm concerned, she should have been the director but, as I said, she's young and lacks experience. It was thought that a production of this scale couldn't be entrusted to her." Clearly Yusuf was the one who waved the money about, but it was Franz who called the tune.

"What kind of films had Müller done previously?"

"Oh, just run-of-the-mill stuff. Fantasy films, love films, et cetera. He's not bad, but he hasn't any films of note to his name. I have a list of the films he's made, and the tapes. I'll give them to you. He didn't ask for much money, which was a point in his favour. Instead of having a first-class, costly, well-known director, we selected first-class people for everything else. We put a very good team together. For instance, Professor Serdar Parlar is advising us. He's an Ottoman historian at Boğaziçi University. And Miss Bauer is a brilliant director... It never really occurred to us that Müller might not be a success."

"Have I got it wrong? Because I thought a film is usually remembered for its director?"

"Well yes, and indeed this was a lifetime opportunity for Müller. But as I said, there wasn't much for the director to do. We had a scenario and we had a team. If we'd brought in Eisenstein, it would have made no difference. Müller was experienced enough to put on

the finishing touches. He wasn't that bad... I mean...
No, not that bad."

"So, as I understand it then, it was because of Petra
that Müller was about to embark on the biggest project
of his life."

"Yes."

"Shouldn't it be the other way round? Doesn't the
director normally choose which star he's going to work
with? For example, Fassbinder always used Hanna
Schygulla in his films."

"If she's famous enough, the star can choose her
director. There's no rule about who chooses whom.
Mr Franz assumed that Miss Vogel didn't want to be
overshadowed by the director. In the film business,
relationships and people get very mixed up. It's difficult
to understand who owes what to whom."

"Why did you go into this business?"

"I told you that. I needed something to do and I
thought film production would be right for me. The
family were going to give me some start-up capital
whatever I did." He frowned and looked at me. "Why?
Do you think being a producer is an odd thing to do?"

"No, no, that's not what I meant. But why this film?
You could have started with another film."

"From a business perspective, it was a sensible project.
And it still is."

His tone of voice suggested that he had not lost all
hope as he continued, "Firstly, box-office revenues in
Turkey are likely to be very high because, as you know,
these days there's a lot of interest in sultanas and so on.
Historical novels are always on the best-seller list, and
Donetti's book has been on best-seller lists all over the
world. I thought his readers would go to the film to see

how it compared. Also, Istanbul is in fashion. Do you think it's mere coincidence that famous artists keep escaping to Istanbul?"

"I think you have a talent for business!"

"I was a financial adviser in Germany. I can't do that here, but I have a feel for finance and projects with a potential for profit. I can smell out money." Given that financial advice was considered a respectable profession in Germany, being reduced to acting as a gangsters' stooge in a questionable film-production business was truly tragic for Yusuf. However, I had no intention of spending my whole day listening to his tear-jerking stories.

"Excuse me, I need to find the toilet," I said. It was no longer any surprise that the moment I rose, the blond henchman appeared.

"You need something, ma'am?" he asked. It seemed that either I was beginning to command more respect, or he had been scolded by the maid for failing to ask how I wanted my coffee. I think it was probably the latter.

"Toilet," I said. Short and to the point.

The henchman leaned forwards, indicating straight ahead with his right arm.

"This way, ma'am." In this household, everybody seemed to use identical words and gestures.

He took me as far as the bathroom door. When I came out, he was polishing one of the mirrors in the entrance hall with his jacket sleeve as he waited for me.

Yusuf was biting his nails and gazing at the Bosphorus when the henchman and I returned.

"This is all really bad," he said, as if talking to himself. "We'll have to start all over again and meanwhile a lot of the money's gone. I haven't worked out our losses

155

yet but… The money's just gone up in smoke. And it's going to continue like that."

"You can still finish the film…" I said, feeling that I was repeating myself like a scratched record.

"We handed out advances, paid hotel bills… It'll be difficult for Phoenix to get through this. Things weren't too brilliant anyway, and now we're suspected of murder. Well, it certainly wasn't me."

"I don't think the Mumcu family will go under from losing a bit of money," I said. I leaned over and picked up my small orange handbag from beside my chair. I was standing with the henchman waiting at my side, despite the fact that I'd been rude to him. "Why is this man a constant fixture at our side?" I asked Yusuf.

"In case we want anything. It's called hospitality." He shrugged his shoulders. "You should know that after living here for thirteen years." He was pleased to be giving me a lesson on local custom and tradition.

"We move in different circles," I said.

He didn't realize I was teasing him. "The class differences here are very marked. We Germans are much more like each other, aren't we? I find it all very confusing," he said.

"Yeah," I said, nodding my head in agreement. I was still standing in the same place. "I'm going. Will you let Mr Mumcu know?" I said in Turkish to the henchman.

"Wait here a moment," said the henchman, hurrying out of the room.

I picked up my cigarettes and lighter from among the plates, put them in my handbag and held out my hand to Yusuf. He jumped up in a state of agitation. He had obviously not understood what I had said to the henchman.

"Are you going? You can't go until my brother-in-law comes," he cried anxiously.

"I'll wait until he comes, don't worry," I said. At that moment, I felt Mesut's breath on my neck.

"Hey, you can't go like that, we're going to eat," he whispered in my ear.

I turned round to face him. We were so close we were almost touching.

"We've only just had breakfast, Mr Mumcu. We'll go out to eat later. I have some business to see to," I said, almost as if I was an important businesswoman.

"In that case, we'll have you collected at eight o'clock this evening," he said. He said something in Kurdish and, without giving me a chance to object, started walking briskly towards the stairs.

"That's all I need," I thought.

7

At seven o'clock, I was sitting on my bed with manicured nails and blow-dried hair, staring at my clothes in the wardrobe. My stomach was churning at the mere thought of going out for a meal with Mesut. At least that morning when we'd had breakfast, I'd had good reason to be there. I was there to speak to Yusuf. But now I was openly going out for a meal with a member of the underworld. And I had much better things to do, such as meet up with Petra and, while I still could, find out where she met Müller and why she had suggested him as director for the film.

When I returned to the shop that afternoon, I found the number for Phoenix Films on the Internet. Introducing myself as Inspector Leyla Batuhan from the Istanbul homicide desk, I spoke to Mr Franz. I doubted that anyone would bother to investigate this telephone conversation but, if they were interested, it would be difficult, even impossible, to trace me. Another advantage of being a reader of crime fiction: I had the bright idea of phoning Franz from Galatasaray Post Office. Throughout our conversation, the only thing that aroused his suspicion was that I spoke German as well as a German. Well, I couldn't do anything about that.

Mr Franz confirmed that, as Yusuf had said, it was Petra who proposed Müller. He didn't know if the two had worked together on a film before, in fact he didn't think they had, but was there anything suspicious about Müller and Petra knowing each other? It was a small world and the film business was even smaller.

I didn't think Franz was the murderer because, along with Mesut and Yusuf, he had a lot to lose. My idea, which had at first seemed so reasonable, that Mesut's gang wanted to use the film to smuggle heroin out of the country and had killed Müller because of a disagreement, no longer seemed viable.

I realized that meant I needed to change my tactics and to focus on who would benefit from Müller's death, but so far nobody appeared to have gained anything from the murder. Then suddenly, a thought occurred to me that made me sit bolt upright. There was someone who had benefited from Müller's death. And that person was the assistant director, Miss Bauer. Had not Mr Franz said that very day that the best person to finish the film was Miss Bauer?

"Our team is competent enough. We can complete the film without having to sign an agreement with another director," he had said.

"Who do you have in mind when you say the team is competent enough?" I had asked.

"We have a competent assistant director in Miss Bauer. She can take over."

Of course, it didn't mean the only person to benefit from that murder was Miss Bauer. However, she had been promoted as a result of it. So, until Miss Bauer was eliminated from my list of suspects, I wasn't going to give up my detective work on this murder case and quietly go back to my former monotonous existence.

Perhaps I should have heard alarm bells at discovering it was Petra who set up Müller as director but, whenever I thought about it, I couldn't help remembering how she'd said with apparent sincerity that there was nothing between them. Could there really have been anything going on between Petra and Müller? Perhaps he cheated on her and they'd had a row… A straightforward crime of passion! I didn't even want to think about the possibility of Petra committing a murder because she'd been deceived, and there was no reason to think Müller was killed because of a quarrel. It was a planned murder, not the result of a moment of anger. Nobody would think "what if we were to have a row", and then go off to their lover's room with three extension cables and a hair-dryer that hadn't been on the market for four years.

As I raised my hand to my mouth to bite off a piece of cuticle, I stopped abruptly. I'd had a manicure that day and now I had to decide on something to wear. I concentrated on my wardrobe again.

It was ten past eight by the time I was dressed and giving myself a final look in the mirror, but the doorbell had still not rung. The situation was clear – Mesut had forgotten our date. Ever since he had talked about going out for dinner that evening, I'd felt nervous about the idea. I hadn't been able to stop thinking about it and what it might lead to.

I consoled myself until eight twenty by smoking and trying to convince myself that he was held up in traffic. By eight twenty-two, I could stand it no longer. At eight twenty-three, I put on my shoes and picked up my bag.

One minute later, I locked the door and went out into the street.

I was too smartly dressed to go just anywhere on my own, so I went to the Cactus Café, where I sat at the bar drinking margaritas. Four of them.

It doesn't take as long as you think to drink four margaritas. At nine fifty, I was back home again. The first thing I did was rush over to the phone. I felt a wave of pleasure sweep over me at seeing the flashing red light signalling the good news that I had a voicemail and that my female pride had been saved. I pressed the *Neue Infos* button. "*Sie haben vier neue Nachrichten,*" said the robotic female voice on the contraption that my mother had brought from Germany on one of her visits.

The first message had been left by Petra immediately after I went out. We hadn't seen each other for two days and she was asking why I hadn't called her.

The second message had been at eight forty-two; it was from the landlord on the top floor to remind me that I hadn't paid that month's rent yet. There was no hurry, but she was worried because I was never late with my rent and she wondered if something was wrong.

Someone rang at nine thirty-five, but put the phone down without leaving a message.

At one minute past ten, my elder brother rang from Göttingen to say that my mother's blood pressure had gone up that day and she'd been taken ill in the street. They'd carried her off to hospital but, according to the doctors, there was nothing to worry about.

I collapsed onto a chair. That was all I needed. While I was worrying about being corrupted by the *mafiosi* over here, my mother was suffering over there in hospital.

I dialled my brother's number with little hope of a reply. However, it was possible his wife had stayed at home rather than go to Berlin to see my mother, and I might get some details from her. I was about to put the phone down after five rings, when my brother answered.

"Hirschel," he said.

"What are you doing there?" I asked.

"Kati!" he said, sounding delighted. "We were in the garden and I didn't hear the phone."

"Didn't you go to Berlin? Or is Mother with you?" I asked.

"No, Mother's in Berlin. They took her to Urban Hospital. Why should I be in Berlin?" I think he was drunk.

"Because Mother's in hospital," I said.

"Oh… no! It's nothing serious. She fell onto her right leg and broke her ankle. With old people, the slightest fall can cause a fracture. Of course there's her blood pressure too. But as you know, she's had that for years anyway. Ute and I are having a barbecue in the garden." Ute is my sister-in-law.

"I'm going to Berlin tomorrow," I said.

"Why?" What kind of question was that?

"To see Mother," I said.

"Have you gone out of your mind?" he said in amazement. "I'm not even going from here."

"But I am going," I said. I'd made my mind up at that moment.

"You've spent too much time over there… We don't do that sort of thing. People here don't all pile on top of each other just because of a slight illness. Living in that hot climate has made you as excitable as they are."

"I'm going to Berlin tomorrow, Schalom. We'll meet up there, if you decide to come," I said.

It always made him angry when I spoke in this tone.

"Fine, you go then," he said. We put our phones down without saying goodbye.

I threw my best clothes on the floor without a second thought, and went to bed without removing my make-up.

At first when I awoke the next morning, I couldn't remember the reason for the nagging worry I was feeling. But not for long. I soon remembered first my mother and then the Müller case, which I seemed unable to shake off. Setting aside thoughts of Müller, I jumped out of bed. The sooner I got moving the better if I was to get on a flight to Berlin.

A pain was gradually spreading from the left side of my head. Telling myself out loud that it would pass, I ran to phone the travel agent.

"It's impossible to find seats on any airline at the moment, Miss Hirschel," said the man at the travel agency when I'd finished speaking.

"I simply have to go. If not today, tomorrow at the latest."

"Well, as you know, Turks working abroad and tourists just keep coming at this time of year. And when they come here, what does that mean? It means they have to go back again. I very much doubt if we'll find a seat, but I'll do another check and get back to you."

"OK. Please do that. I'll be at home," I said.

"I can tell you there's no chance of finding a seat on a charter flight, but I'll have a look at the scheduled flights."

"Yes, if you would. And see if there are any indirect flights. I definitely have to go," I said firmly.

I put the telephone down and rushed off to the bathroom. The face that looked back at me in the mirror over the washbasin resembled that of a Venezuelan who had just learned she'd been crowned Miss World. I had mascara and eye shadow running all down my cheeks. I plunged into the shower.

The ring of the telephone resounded throughout the whole apartment, but I only heard it when I turned off the shower. It had to be the travel agent. Wrapping myself in a towel, I ran to the phone taking care not to slip. It was Yılmaz.

"Did you forget? Today's Saturday," he said, without even giving me the chance to say hello.

"Yılmaaz! Something terrible has happened. Where are you? Come over here and we'll have breakfast, and…"

He interrupted, saying, "I'm in the café next to the mosque, where else would I be? I'll be there in five minutes," he said.

We sat with our legs propped up on the balcony railing and, on Yılmaz's instructions, were enjoying our tea. I'd been telling him what had been happening to me over the past ten days. Not everything of course, just what was necessary. Then the phone rang. I had a strong urge to escape any further disaster by fleeing to a mountain village with no telephone connection. If such a place still exists.

This time it was the travel agent telling me there was a Turkish Airlines flight at thirteen forty-five the next day and asking if I wanted it.

"Yes, of course," I said.

"When will you be returning?"

"In a week's time, maybe ten days. It might be less, but not more than ten days."

"In that case, I'll make the ticket out for two weeks, although a one-week ticket would be cheaper... At the moment, Turkish Airlines costs more than Lufthansa. A fifteen-day return ticket is 450 dollars, just so you know. Naturally, they can't find clients at these prices. It's not for nothing that everyone says Turkish Airlines should be privatized. Their losses are carried by all of us. In the old days, there were special workers' tickets, but not any more. Although we couldn't have got you a worker's ticket anyway, so nothing's changed as far as you're concerned."

"The money's not important. My mother's ill and I definitely have to go," I said.

"Oh my God, I'm so sorry, Miss Hirschel. What's wrong with her?"

That's how Turks are. They always try to join in any problem, whether it's necessary or not.

"I don't know yet. They've taken her to hospital, but I couldn't get through by phone. I'll find out when I get there," I said, trying to keep things brief. "How late are you open? I'll come and collect the ticket," I added.

"There's no need to come here, you can pick it up at the airport tomorrow. You have enough on your plate at the moment, so don't bother coming here. I'll have your ticket left at the Turkish Airlines desk in the airport."

"And the money? How will I pay?"

"We'll sort it out when you get back, don't worry about it, ma'am."

"No way, I'll transfer the money to your account. Tell me how much 450 dollars comes to in Turkish lira."

"The banks are closed on Saturdays, Miss Hirschel."

"I'll send it via the Internet," I said. The agent's respect for me went up a notch when he heard I did Internet banking and, after he had told me about his daughter, who was a third-year medical student and had become an Internet hotshot, he gave me his account number.

I was to fly the next day.

I returned to the balcony, where I found Yılmaz buried in the newspapers.

"Your Mumcu has been arrested again," he said when he saw me. "But it's not in connection with the murder this time," he added.

I didn't enquire why he'd been arrested, but merely asked, "When did that happen?"

"Yesterday evening. They raided Mumcu Transport after a tip-off and found two unlicensed weapons. He spent the night in the cells. This time Mesut's had it. His bail conditions mean he'll probably go back to jail," he said.

"Who knows? Maybe," I said, trying to sound indifferent. But I immediately created an excuse to escape to the kitchen. "Shall we have some coffee?" I asked.

Yılmaz looked at his watch.

"I can't. I have to be at the office at one o'clock. There's a meeting today. We're working like crazy."

"Have there been any redundancies yet?" I asked. The last time we'd spoken, he'd said they were going to start letting people go.

He appeared irritated by my question and headed for the door. I followed him.

"So far they haven't got rid of anyone, but we all have the sword of Damocles hanging over us. I've lost the taste for this business. If I hadn't sunk all my savings in the stock market, I'd have settled down in a village on the Aegean long ago. I'm too old for this sort of thing."

He wished me a safe journey, kissed me on both cheeks and hurried off.

I made myself a large cup of Turkish coffee and sat at my desk. First, I went onto the Internet and transferred the rent money to the landlady's account and the money for the airline ticket to the travel agent. While on the Internet, I tried reading what the papers had written about Mesut, but the computer was so slow I soon gave up. It made more sense to go and buy a paper from the shop.

After I'd finished on the Internet, I called Petra. She wasn't in her room, so I left a message. I was just thinking about who else I should be calling when the telephone rang.

"Are you still angry with me?" asked Lale.

"No, I'm not angry," I said curtly, and blurted out what had happened to my mother.

"So, you're going tomorrow. What time's the flight?"

"Thirteen forty-five."

"Shall I take you to the airport? Would you like that? I can go to the office from there."

"You mean you'll go to work at two o'clock in the afternoon?" She was at work by eight every morning, including Sundays. She only took one day off a week, which was Saturday.

"Yes," she said.

"What's happened?" I asked anxiously. Her closest friend's mother being in hospital was not reason enough for Lale to be late for work. There was definitely something else.

"Nothing's happened. Or maybe it has. Perhaps I've been smitten by the curses of all those people I've sacked over the last four months on the pretext of an economic crisis. I'm fed up of this business, Kati. I've had enough. I wish I'd never come back from New York."

"Why don't you come over to my place and we can go out somewhere together," I said. I'd never heard her say she regretted coming back from New York before. She was clearly at the end of her tether.

"I can't come over, I have to sort out my study. Everything's piled up all over the place. I must have some order. When my head's so mixed up, at least my surroundings must be in order. You come over to me." I could tell that she didn't want to be alone. I was used to Lale's only-child idiosyncrasies.

"I need to get ready for my journey tomorrow, and I want to see Petra. It's not possible for me to come there," I said.

"In that case, let's meet early before we go to the airport; it'll give us a chance to talk."

As soon as I put the receiver down, the phone rang again. This time it was Petra.

"I'm in the pool. You called me. What lovely weather, hot and sunny. I really needed a holiday like this," she said. She spoke as if she was glad that Müller had been killed.

"What are you doing today?" I asked.

"I'm not doing anything in particular during the day. In the evening, I'm going out for dinner with the film crew."

I told Petra that my mother had been taken to hospital and I was going to Berlin. Cunningly, I added, "I'll come and join you and the film crew for dinner this evening, so I'll see you there. I haven't got time now because I have to pack."

"Well, I don't know. Might it not seem a bit strange?" she said.

"Are you invited to someone's house?"

"No, we're going to a typical Turkish restaurant."

"So what's strange about that? Restaurants are public places, anyone can come," I said.

Everyone was going to meet at seven o'clock at the Noel Baba Hotel in Tarlabaşı where they were all staying, except for Petra. "Come over to me if you like and we can go there together. The hotel is very close to where I live," I said, and told her to write down my address.

It took half an hour to spell everything out letter by letter to her. "Why is this address so long?" she asked, sounding bored.

"Because it's not just the address, I've given you directions as well. You can give that piece of paper to the taxi driver."

"Why do I need directions? You only needed to give me the address," she said with German naivety.

"What do you think Istanbul taxi drivers are? Unless you're going to a mosque, police station or hospital, you won't get anywhere in Istanbul by just giving them a street name. Taxi drivers don't even know the name of the district they live in," I said.

"Don't be ridiculous," she said.

"Well, try it this evening when you come to me. Just say Tavukuçmaz Street to the driver, and let's see if he can get you here," I said. "But be careful, if you cross the

Bosphorus Bridge to the Asian side, it takes a long time to get back."

"That's exactly how you used to be, you haven't changed at all. You love to exaggerate."

"OK, you'll see whether I'm caricaturing taxi drivers, or whether they do that for themselves," I said, confident that I'd be proved right.

"We'll see," she said resolutely.

Going out for dinner that evening meant that, before I left for Berlin, I would have spoken to the only suspect on my list and also seen the other crew members: I felt like a girl of ten, or perhaps fifteen.

Next I called Pelin. I was going to have to leave my business completely in her hands during my absence.

"Don't worry, I'll manage. The important thing is for your mother to get better," said Pelin.

I asked her what she wanted from Berlin. It's a Turkish custom. You always ask friends if they want anything whenever you go anywhere. And even if they're really hankering after some duty-free perfume, the friends will reply, "You just come back in one piece, that's all I want."

Pelin was exactly the same.

After clearing up the breakfast things and filling the dishwasher, I went into the bedroom to pack my suitcase. I was about to put in T-shirts and shorts, but suddenly realized I had no idea what the weather would be like in Berlin. All I knew was that it was unlikely to be as hot as Istanbul. I went back to the study to look up the weather forecast for the next few days.

As I thought, the weather in Berlin was dreadful and set to continue like that. There would be a couple of sunny days towards the end of the month but I had no intention of being in Berlin that long, if things went to plan.

I threw aside the T-shirts and shorts and pulled out my red jacket, some sweatshirts and a pair of velvet trousers from the back of my wardrobe. I didn't need to dress as smartly in Berlin as I did in Istanbul. In the metros over there most people look as if they've run away from a nuthouse.

Once I'd packed my large bag of cosmetics and my suitcase, my travel preparations were complete. Petra wouldn't arrive for another two hours, provided she gave the written directions to the driver. It would be four hours if she didn't.

I went out to buy a newspaper.

Page three of the magazine section, which was devoted to news of disasters, was covered with photographs of Mesut in the company of various singers. The accompanying reports told me nothing that Yılmaz hadn't already read out to me. It suddenly occurred to me to call the reporter who worked for Lale's newspaper, but I immediately thought better of the idea. It would only get back to Mesut. However, I had a burning desire to phone somebody, in a way that only an *İstanbullu* would understand, so I dialled Batuhan's mobile number.

He didn't sound pleased to hear my voice.

"Hello," he said coldly.

"How are you?"

"I'm working. I'm very busy."

"Then I won't disturb you."

"Good."

I put the telephone down.

I wasn't surprised at his reaction. I was old enough to have experience of, and even theories about, the behaviour of rejected men. The biggest difference between men and women facing rejection is that men waste no time in showing their true nature. On the other hand, women maintain their composure for a while, thinking that maybe he hasn't really rejected them, that there's merely some misunderstanding... The result is that women only reach the revenge stage after the fourth rejection has been confirmed, whereas men become vindictive at the slightest setback.

Also from experience, I've learned that you can't take revenge on someone who doesn't care about you, whereas it's easy to take revenge on someone who loves you – all you have to do is commit suicide.

Take Batuhan for example. How could he take his revenge on me, given that he was incapable of making me feel bad enough to commit suicide?

1. He could wake me up with telephone calls in the middle of the night and then put the phone down without speaking.

2. He could put a dead mouse in front of my shop and leave a note saying "Dirty infidel, get out of our country", and follow this up by throwing stones through my shop window.

3. He could claim that I'd murdered Müller and have me arrested.

4. He could plant a bag of heroin in my apartment, car or shop and report me to the police.

The most realistic of these, actually the only realistic one, was the first. But I'd received at least six different kinds of silent phone calls, so one more wasn't going to cast a shadow over my life.

All Turks, regardless of class, age or gender, are used to taking revenge with silent telephone calls, and everyone has their own style. One will put the telephone down the moment you lift the receiver and before you can even say "Hallo". Another will wait until you make yourself hoarse from shouting "Hallo" down the phone. There are other types who make you listen to music, whistle tunes down the line or fake orgasms… Anyone wanting to live in Turkey has to get used to these strange Turkish customs. I've become used to them. I always unplug the phone before I go to bed, provided I'm not blind drunk or involved in solving a murder.

The telephone rang as I waited in the kitchen for the water to boil to make myself some green tea. I ran to the study. I keep talking about the telephone, so I should explain that the only one in my apartment was in my study.

"Is Miss Hirschel there?" It was a man whose voice I didn't recognize but who, according to my friend Mithat's theory about Kurdish accents, was probably from Diyarbakir.

"Yes, it's me."

"Sorry to disturb you. I'm ringing on behalf of Mr Mumcu."

"Yes?"

"He said he'd promised to see you… But some urgent business came up and he couldn't make it. He wanted me to let you know; he'll call when he can."

"Thank you," I said.

Surely Mesut must have realized I'd see the news about his arrest? I went into the kitchen repeating to myself, "Some urgent business came up."

Having someone like Mesut, who could talk with such ease about having people killed, loose on the streets was no good to anyone. The sooner he was locked up, the more lives would be saved. And from my point of view, it was a good thing he'd been sent back to jail before we went out for dinner.

Just then the doorbell rang. I burned my hand as I took the kettle off the stove. I hate being in a rush!

I ran to the sitting-room window sucking the scalded little finger of my right hand. Petra was standing in front of the door to the apartment building. She'd arrived early. I hadn't even had the chance to drink a peaceful cup of tea.

Grumbling about this, I pressed the button to open the front door.

I was still licking my little finger as I watched Petra pant her way up the stairs.

"Since we're spending the evening over here, I thought I'd spend the day wandering around the Taksim Square area. I'm exhausted. But there was so much to see. I walked as far as your shop. Today's little city tour was more than enough for me."

"Come inside," I said, turning back towards the kitchen. The water that had been boiling away was now the right temperature for making green tea. I put tea leaves into a glass teapot, filled it with water and put another cup on the tray. As I walked towards the balcony, the sound of Petra's amazed voice could be heard from the sitting room.

"How big your apartment is. And your street is so lovely…"

"Come onto the balcony, then we can talk without shouting," I said. The balcony was also the coolest place to sit.

Petra sat on the chair where Yılmaz had sat that morning; I sat opposite her.

"Istanbul is such a tiring city; the crowds are quite overwhelming. Today I found myself wondering what it would be like to live here…" said Petra. She seemed to feel a need to correct herself and added, "But I'm sure if you live here all the time, you get used to it."

"Even if you get used to the crowds in Istanbul, there are other things that get to you," I said.

"What for example?"

"Turkish politics, the economic crisis, corruption, bank charges…"

I said this with considerable anger and Petra stared at me in surprise.

I was unable to speak in a normal tone of voice, so I continued in a whisper, "Ever since this morning, I've been calming down friends who want to escape from here. The political and economic problems have hit everyone." My outburst of anger surprised me also. "It seems to have affected me more than I thought," I said.

As each new crisis unfolded, I'd thought I was less sensitive than Turks were to Turkey's problems. I'd tell myself that while Istanbul was certainly my city, Turkey wasn't my country. The difference between me and Lale, Yılmaz, Pelin and other friends was not the strength of our feelings but the extent. Once I'd said to Lale, "You love a part of Turkey which is Istanbul, whereas I only love Istanbul. But I do understand you. It's the same as me loving Cihangir because it's in Istanbul… If Cihangir had been in Bonn, I wouldn't have liked it." My love for Istanbul had nothing to do with Turkey. I loved Istanbul food, Istanbul songs, Istanbul Turkish and the Cihangir district of Istanbul.

Petra hadn't realized I'd become so distracted, and she continued talking.

"I bought a Turkish paper yesterday and it was in German. Turkey's situation looks pretty hopeless, doesn't it?"

"Take no notice," I said. "I've been living here thirteen years and I've never known the situation to be hopeful."

I licked my scalded finger once again and poured the over-brewed tea.

"You weren't really in a relationship with Kurt Müller, were you?" I asked Petra as I passed her tea.

"Why are you asking that again? I told you before that I wasn't, didn't I?"

"They say you suggested Müller for that job, that's why…"

"Who's saying that?" Was her surprise at how I had obtained that information, or at how such lies could be made up against her?

"Some people from Mumcu Productions," I said. For some reason, I didn't want her to know that I'd gone as far as telephoning Mr Franz in Germany.

She fiddled with the cross and chain that hung around her neck and looked at me thoughtfully.

"You mean the man you called from my room?"

"No, someone who works with him. A German called Yusuf."

"Joseph?"

"He's a German Muslim called Yusuf."

"Ah, I understand what you mean. I know him. Was that his name, Yossof? OK, so what did he tell you?"

"He said it was you who found Müller."

"That's true. I found Kurt. But what if I did?"

"Well, you knew each other from before."

"Yes, we knew each other. But I know a lot of people, Kati. I don't get into a relationship with everyone I know. The producer sent me the screenplay about a year ago. For the first time in years, I saw a part for myself in it. I'm no longer considered young." As she said this, she unbuttoned her blouse and pinched the spare tyre around her waist.

"As we get older, it's not just the energy that goes; the body deteriorates as well. There'd be no problem if I looked as young as you, but unfortunately I show my age. In fact, I look even older than my age. It must be true when they say blondes deteriorate faster than brunettes. I'm sure you realize that leading roles don't just drop through my letterbox every week. Naturally I did whatever I could to get the film made. They needed an experienced director who wouldn't ask for too much money. I knew someone who fitted that description, so I brought them together."

What she was saying sounded convincing. In an era when being young and remaining young is exalted like never before, a woman's greatest treasures are a pair of legs without cellulite and skin without wrinkles, aren't they? Whatever her role or profession. So a film star is obviously affected by all that more than the rest of us.

"You mean the reason you suggested Müller wasn't that you were in a relationship with him?"

"How many more times do I have to say it, I wasn't in a relationship with Kurt. He may have liked me, and he may have said so to various people, but…" – she leaned across the table and looked me straight in the eyes – "…there was nothing between us. Anyway, he wasn't my type."

Her last comment disturbed me. It was the sort of thing a fifteen-year-old girl might say.

"What do you mean, he wasn't your type?"

"Unsuccessful, incompetent even…" If I hadn't interrupted her, she would have said more.

"If he was unsuccessful and incompetent, why did you suggest him for this film? Why did you want him to direct a film that was so important to you if he was no good?"

"The reason's simple. The director wouldn't over-shadow me and my name would have top billing. As for the producers…" She laughed like a star posing for the cameras. "They had as much experience as Kurt, but they were looking for someone cheap."

Yusuf had said more or less the same thing when we spoke. Clearly, the film world was a much stranger place than I could have imagined.

We didn't mention the film or Kurt Müller again until we left the apartment to meet the film crew for dinner.

When Petra and I entered the lobby of the Noel Baba Hotel in Tarlabaşı, I looked very young with my hair in a ponytail and no make-up, or that's how they describe such women in novels. Actually it wasn't my intention to appear young, but I just hadn't bothered to take my make-up bag out of my suitcase.

The loud group of Germans in the lobby fell silent when they saw us.

"This is my friend, Kati Hirschel," said Petra.

One man in the group, who was completely nonde-script apart from his almost white blond hair, held out his hand without standing up. "Hallo, I'm Gust," he said.

The others told me their names without shaking hands and, before long, lost interest in me and continued their noisy conversation. There were nine of them, all men except for two women, neither of whom claimed to be called Bauer.

"Where shall we go?" I asked Gust. I was perching on the edge of the two-seater lobby sofa on which he was sprawled.

"We have a guide for tonight, a journalist friend of mine who lives in Istanbul." He was clearly proud of his friend's profession.

"Otto has been here for two years. He chose the place we're going to. He's just gone out with Annette to find a chemist." Gust looked at his watch. "They'll be back soon."

"Who's Annette?" I asked, hoping that her surname was Bauer.

"Annette Bauer, the film's assistant director." He quickly corrected himself, saying, "Or rather from today, I should say the director."

So, Miss Bauer was now officially the director of this film and I was about to meet her.

"Where does your journalist friend work? I might know him because I live in Istanbul too."

"Otto writes for *Westdeutsche Zeitung*," he said, as if he was talking about the President of the United States rather than a mere journalist. He looked at me carefully as if he'd only just understood what I said, and added, "Did you say you live in Istanbul?"

"Yes."

"Are you a journalist too?"

"I have a bookshop that sells crime fiction," I said.

"Did you come here to sell books?"

"No, I was already living here. I changed jobs a few times before deciding to become a bookseller."

"Interesting," he said. "Very interesting."

"Do you mean being a bookseller?"

"No, I mean living here, even though you don't have to. I don't understand how anyone can live in a country that has a human-rights problem. Don't you worry that something might happen to you? And there's been a big rise in thieving and pickpocketing since the economic crisis. Otto told us to take good care of our bags and money. There isn't a person left in Istanbul who hasn't had their bag stolen."

"In Germany, a foreigner is attacked about every four or five days and skinheads kill people in the middle of the street, but there are still foreigners living there," I said angrily.

Instead of answering me, Gust turned away. I studied his profile and decided to soften my words a little. It wouldn't do me any good to get on the wrong side of this man.

"I like Istanbul," I said.

Again he said nothing, but he turned back towards me.

To change the subject, I said, "When does filming start?"

"This tragic event has shocked us all of course," he said. I could have sworn that his face showed not the slightest hint of any shock. You'd never have guessed from the loud conversation of this film crew that one of their colleagues had been found dead just a few days before. But that was another matter.

"Of course it has," I said. I was on such good form that day that I would have been a match for any politician.

"This break has been good for us. The actors have got into the atmosphere of the city, we've got the technical team and extras sorted out, and we've got to know each other…" He smirked and added, "It was decided today that Miss Bauer will direct the film." He suddenly realized that she wasn't back yet. Turning to the others, he pointed to his wristwatch and asked, "Where have they got to, for God's sake?"

A pink-faced German grinned where he sat in front of three empty beer bottles, and said, "Is there some dark spirit following our directors around, do you think?"

Everyone in the group laughed heartily at this joke. From her chair, Petra was watching me out of the corner of her eye, so I quickly changed my withering look to one of my friendly expressions and laughed too.

"If you find out where we're going, we could leave them a note and go," I said to Gust. I couldn't wait to get out of that unpleasant lobby.

"I already know where we're going," said Gust. He stood up and rummaged in his trouser pockets, pulled out a crumpled piece of paper and slowly read out what was written on it.

"Has-seer Restaurant."

Petra felt compelled to make a statement to the others.

"Kati lives in Istanbul. She knows the city really well."

One of the women in the group smiled and said, "Oh, how lucky you are. Istanbul is the most beautiful city I've ever seen."

"Have you seen any other cities apart from Frankfurt?" asked one of the others.

Everybody burst into laughter at this joke.

"In that case, let's go," I said. "The place we're going to is very close to the hotel anyway."

Gust's journalist friend had chosen the Hasır Restaurant in Tarlabaşı, a place that is frequented by everyone's tourist friends as a typical Turkish restaurant, or rather café.

"Let's pay the bill," said a second pink face who was sitting next to the first pink face. He shouted louder than ever in order to get the waiter's attention.

Everyone sitting in the lobby was looking at this man crying out, "Hallo!!! Halloo!!" as if he was gripped by hysteria. The other hotel residents and I breathed a sigh of relief when the waiter finally rushed up out of breath, thinking some disaster had happened.

"The bill," said the second pink face in German. "Separately."

"Do you want the bill, sir?" asked the waiter in English.

"Don't you know German?" asked the man, again in German.

The waiter knew enough German to understand this question. "*Nein*," he said.

I thought it was time for me to intervene.

"They want the bill, and they'll pay separately," I said in Turkish.

The waiter turned to me, pleased to have found someone he could communicate with.

"We'll put it on their bills, ma'am. They're all hotel clients."

I translated the waiter's suggestion to the others.

"No way," said Gust. "My friend said they might cheat us. We'll pay now."

"They want to pay now," I said to the waiter, but he didn't need me to translate everything that Gust said.

"Fine," said the waiter. He told Gust what was on his bill.

"The gentleman had two beers. Five million Turkish lira."

"Two beers, five million," I said to Gust.

Gust got up again, rummaged in his pockets and pulled out ten marks, which he held out to the waiter. The waiter looked at the money and said, "We don't take marks."

"They don't take marks," I said to Gust. "Haven't you got any Turkish lira?"

"No," said Gust. Still holding out the money, he said, "Can they change it at reception?"

"Maybe, but you can't pay the bill with marks."

"What nonsense," said Gust. "In that case, he can change this note at reception."

One of the pink faces supported Gust, saying, "Yes, he can change it at reception."

Gust was still waving the ten-mark note about as if he was showing a dog a bone. I was in the process of deciding whose mouth I'd stuff that money down while the waiter stood anxiously without moving a muscle.

Suddenly, a bearded man appeared next to us out of nowhere.

"Are you wanting to pay the bill in marks?" he asked in German.

Gust was so pleased to be able to explain without an interpreter that he jumped in first.

"Yes," he said.

"This is Turkey," said the bearded man. "Bills are paid in Turkish lira here."

"But they change marks at reception," said Gust, clinging to his only argument. However, his tone of voice suggested that he was starting to cave in.

"Would I try to pay a bill in Germany with Turkish lira?" said the bearded man, who had clearly been irritated by the Germans on an earlier occasion.

The group threw sheepish glances at each other.

"But…" said Gust, trying once more.

"No buts. Here bills are paid in Turkish lira." Just as he was leaving, he turned and said, "And don't talk so loudly. It's disturbing for us."

He walked away, sat down in an armchair in the far corner and buried himself in a newspaper.

The woman who had just said she loved Istanbul held out a five-million-lira note to the waiter.

"A coffee," she said in English.

The waiter took the money and, not having understood the argument that had taken place in German, looked at me questioningly and asked, "What happened, ma'am?"

"Never mind," I said. "They're going to pay the bill in Turkish lira."

We left a note for Miss Bauer and Otto at reception and left the hotel. It was a ten-minute walk to the Hasır café.

"We try to make everywhere we go conform to our own little world, don't we?" said the woman who loved Istanbul. She had skilfully moved away from her crew and was walking next to me.

Smiling, I said, "You mean like paying bills in marks?"

"Yes, that's an example. The same goes for drinking beer and eating sausages. It makes me shiver to see how

German stereotypes are true. I don't know if you've ever been to Mallorca. They've established a small German province there. You'd never know you were in another country. The weather is warmer of course and the sun shines all the time. But that's all."

"Have you ever lived abroad?" I asked. In my experience, only those who have lived abroad have what it takes to criticize their own people, especially in the case of Germans.

She turned her head quickly towards me. "You can tell, can't you?" she said. "I was married to an Egyptian. He worked in foreign affairs and we travelled a lot. When we divorced, I went back to my old work. This film's my first big job." She shook her head and continued, "As you see, I don't have much luck. Look what happened."

What more could I ask for? The conversation had come round to exactly where I wanted without me saying anything.

"You mean the murder." I said. That wasn't a question. "If you ask me, the people in your group don't seem very upset by it."

"Nobody knew Müller very well. Only…" She stopped, unsure whether to finish her sentence. She suddenly seemed to be taking great care not to trip over the uneven pavement, a popular feature of Istanbul city planning. Her eyes didn't stray from her feet to look at me for even a second.

"You mean Petra?" I said.

She looked at me carefully and said, "So you know too."

"If you mean that it was Petra who arranged the job for Müller, then yes, I've heard about it. But a relationship between them was out of the ques—"

I had difficulty stopping myself from shouting at a man who bumped into my shoulder as he passed by.

"Petra says there was no relationship between them," I continued, gossiping to this woman I'd known for five minutes as if she was an old friend. It wasn't something to be proud of.

The woman went back to studying her feet. "I didn't think they were in a relationship either," she said.

That was interesting.

"Why?" I asked, leaning forward in order to see her face.

She put her arm through mine, brought her mouth close to my ear so that the others wouldn't hear, and continued talking in a low voice. We had fallen to the back of the group so there wasn't anyone nearby to hear us anyway.

"I saw how she behaved towards Müller. At Berlin airport, Müller put his arm round her waist and she pushed his hand away with an expression of real revulsion, and immediately moved away. And after we arrived in Istanbul, I saw them together having breakfast. I… I don't want to exaggerate, but I have a sense for that sort of thing. A woman would never behave that way towards a man she was having, or was going to have, a relationship with. I'm certain there was nothing between them." She pursed her lips and added, "I don't think there ever would have been."

"But there's no proof that nothing was going on between Petra and the murdered man," I said.

"Proof?" She lifted her head and looked at me as if to ask what more did I want.

Gust, the natural leader of the group, was calling to us from in front. I shouted back that we hadn't yet reached the Hasır café.

"OK, so who do you think did this murder?" I asked the woman. I felt sure she'd have an opinion about it.

"I don't think it was anyone in the film crew. It must have been someone from outside. Perhaps he called for a prostitute that night." She stopped and sighed. "You know, he was just the sort of man to go with prostitutes. Maybe he didn't pay the woman and she got angry and psht..." As she said this, she lifted her left arm and opened her fingers as if she was dropping an object to the ground.

"Why do you think it wasn't one of the crew?" I asked.

"Why not?" she said. "You can say many things about the crew, but none of them has it in them," she said finally.

"So you had a hunch..."

"Yes, a hunch." She stopped. "But don't make light of my hunches."

I smiled.

"You mean it was simply gossip that Petra and Müller were having an affair?" I asked. This matter kept preying on my mind.

"In my view, yes."

"Who do you think started this gossip?"

"I don't know who started it, but they managed to persuade the whole crew that it was true." Taking hold of my arm again, she smiled grimly and said, "See, even you were persuaded." She wasn't bad-looking really but, despite being no more than four or five years older than me, her dress style and mannerisms were already making her look old.

I looked around in an attempt to get away from all this gossip and saw that we'd passed the Hasır.

The café, known to Istanbul regulars as "the Hasır next to the police station", was in a Tarlabaşı basement that was reached by a low-ceilinged flight of stairs. When anyone asked why this basement was preferable to the evening cool of the cafés and fish restaurants on the Bosphorus, clients always gave the same reply as if by agreement: they served great *meze* at the Hasır.

As soon as the head waiter saw the large group of tourists at the door, he waved his hand at his small army of *commis* waiters and ordered them to pull some tables together.

We finally managed to sit down and to my horror I found myself sitting between the two pink faces. I made no objection because the chair opposite was vacant and I hoped Miss Bauer would soon come and sit there.

By the time Otto, the German newspaper corre-spondent in Turkey, and Miss Bauer appeared, we were halfway through our *meze* course. The pink faces on either side of me were already drunk because of the beers they'd had earlier at the hotel. Miss Bauer didn't sit opposite me as I'd hoped, but went to sit next to Gust at the other end of the table and, from what I could hear, immediately proceeded to give an account of why they were late. Even someone without well-developed hunches could see these two were more than just friends.

I had no choice but to start up a conversation with Otto, who had sat down opposite me.

"Gust told me you live in Istanbul," I said.

"It would be more true to say that I work in Istanbul," he said. Was he saying that Istanbul was no place to live?

"Don't you like it here?"

"No, not at all. How could I?" he said.

"I like it," I said. He laughed disdainfully.

"You don't live in Istanbul, that's why. I think it's a very attractive place for tourists and the food is wonderful."

"I'm not a tourist. I've lived here for thirteen years," I said.

"Thirteen years?"

I nodded. "And I intend to live here for another thirteen years."

He didn't seem very keen to argue with me because he kept his head down and studied his plate of *meze* until the waiter asked him what he wanted to drink.

When I heard him ask the waiter in English for a glass of white wine, I realized this was my chance.

"It must be difficult to understand a country and write about it without knowing the language," I blurted out. I didn't care; making fun of him had to be better than trying to chat to the two pink faces on either side of me.

"We can't learn the language of every country we go to," he said. "We move from one country to another every few years. Which language should we learn?"

"But if you don't know the language, you can't read the newspapers and you can't sit in cafés talking to people."

"I work with an interpreter," he said, making a last attempt to end the conversation.

"If you knew Turkish, you'd like Istanbul." I said this in a romantic tone and, with the same romantic voice, added, "As an Istanbul poet said, anyone who doesn't love Istanbul doesn't know the meaning of love..."

Then I suddenly became serious.

"Did you write the articles about the murder?"

The man was trying to find a link between the different topics and my quick changes of mood.

"We haven't met, have we?" he said finally.

I extended my hand across the plate of sardines that lay between us and said, "I learnt from Gust that your name is Otto. I'm Kati Hirschel," I said.

"Otto Frisch," he said. He shook my hand a few times with his large fingers. "Call me Otto," he said.

"And you can call me Kati," I said.

I suddenly realized everyone at the table had their head turned towards me. The waiter was standing with pen and paper in hand, waiting to take the order. I signalled with my hand towards Otto and turned to my left.

"Shall we eat fish?" said the woman who liked Istanbul, leaning forward to look at me.

"I think so," I said, and embarked on a conversation with the waiter about which fish was in season.

When I decided that we'd eat gilt-headed bream, the others were still staring at me in silence.

"I don't know the German name of the fish I ordered," I said.

"We'll see what it is when it arrives," said the woman who liked Istanbul, leaning back in her chair.

Otto patted the front pocket of his shirt and said, "I have a dictionary, let's see what it is." There was no chance of him producing Steuerwald's thousand-page Turkish/German dictionary out of that shirt pocket, and in fact he got out a small yellow plastic-covered Langenscheidt and waved it in the air.

"Don't bother looking, it's not in there," I said.

"How do you spell it?" he asked obstinately.

I started to spell out the word for him.

"You're right, it's not in here," he said, after looking for it optimistically. Meanwhile the pink faces, who had been silent for a while, had started to talk to each other in a spray of spittle.

"Would you like to change places with me?" I asked the one on my right.

This meant I was one seat further away from the rest of the team, but at least I had escaped from the beery breath of the two pink faces.

Again I asked Otto, "Did you write the murder article?"

"Yes. Why do you ask?"

"Then I've read what you wrote," I said.

"What I wrote wasn't anything much. I doubt if there'll be any further developments to justify writing more about it," he said.

"Why?" I asked. Was I the only one who hadn't given up hope over this?

"No reason at all. It's an unsolvable murder. I had an interview today with the inspector who is investigating this murder; it'll be published tomorrow. He says they don't have any leads and they're preparing to close the file. At this rate, that will happen in a couple of days."

"Who did you speak to?"

"Do you know him?" he asked, as he tried to swallow a mouthful of sardines.

"I know someone on the homicide desk."

He took out a notepad from the same shirt pocket that contained the dictionary and started turning the pages.

"Batuhan Önal was his name. Do you know him?"

"No," I said calmly. "Does he say they can't solve this murder?"

"Of course he's not saying that. That's what I inferred from what he said. It's a strange business; they're absolutely refusing to let the German police get involved in the investigation. If they think they can't solve it, then why don't they accept help? I don't understand."

"Didn't you just say that there aren't any leads?"

"Yes."

"If there aren't any leads, what could the German police do?"

"Well that's just it. If the German police were here, they'd find a lead."

I had difficulty stopping myself punching the air and laughing out loud.

"How nice that you think the German police are so resourceful," I said. "My knowledge of German police is that they are famous for killing the hostage in order to catch the hostage-taker."

Otto put the notepad back in his pocket and shook his head angrily. He clearly didn't approve of my anti-German attitude.

"Who do you think the murderer is?" I asked.

"I don't like that sort of speculation," he said sullenly.

"Make a guess," I said. "Don't you ever play the lottery?"

That made him very uneasy and he didn't answer. Even the bream garnished with rocket, which he swallowed without chewing, was not enough to dispel the rage he felt towards me.

As I ate my fish in a silence that confused even me, it dawned on me that I wouldn't be able to talk to Miss Bauer while she was sitting at one end of the three tables pushed together and I was at the other. As the plates were being cleared away, I suggested going for a drink at a nearby café. Most of the crew said they wanted to go back to the hotel because they were tired and had had enough for one day. Petra was among those who didn't feel like carrying on.

I set off walking through the back streets of Beyoğlu towards the Cactus Café with Gust, Miss Bauer, Otto and the woman who liked Istanbul, whose name I finally found out to be Miss Wolff. As we walked, I acted as a guide and provided a running commentary: it was doubtful we'd find a place at the Cactus, but we were going to try and, if not there, we'd go to one of the six thousand or so cafés or bars in the vicinity of Beyoğlu – over ten thousand if you counted the unlicensed places.

A second good thing happened that day, after finding a ticket to Berlin, which was that despite the crowds of people we found a table at the Cactus that was just being vacated. It didn't escape Miss Wolff's notice that I was greeted as an old friend by Vahit the barman.

The moment we sat down, she said, "You're clearly well known here."

I smiled modestly.

Miss Bauer drew back her bright-red hair and said, "You're Petra's bookseller friend, aren't you? I saw you at the airport the day we arrived in Istanbul."

"You have an excellent memory," I said. It was quite something to pick me out in that crowd and then recognize me later.

It was Miss Wolff who raised the subject of the murder. Otto saw his opportunity and repeated what he had previously said to me at dinner. As he spoke, I watched Miss Bauer's face for some kind of reassurance. That woman was an extremely cold-hearted killer, or else my hunch, like all my other hunches, was wrong. And that was something I found it very difficult to get my head around. Her face was completely expressionless. For once I decided to try out a shock tactic.

"Actually, the only person to benefit from this murder is you," I said to Miss Bauer, as soon as Otto had stopped speaking.

The four of them spun their heads round towards me and I sensed I needed to do something to defuse the situation.

"Only joking," I said. "Just thinking out loud... You misunderstood me."

Miss Wolff laughed.

"You can't really say that Annette has benefited from the murder; she's had to take on a whole lot of extra responsibilities," she said.

"Why not? She's ended up being promoted," I said, as if the woman was not there.

"Aren't you oversimplifying things?" asked Otto.

"Yes, indeed," said Gust.

"Well, it's simple," I said. "Murder is simple. We're talking about killing a man for honour, money, love, revenge or sex. What's complicated about that?"

"The murderer might have had another motive," said Otto. He thought he'd cornered me.

"Give me another motive," I said.

As he thought about that, it occurred to me that the murderer might have had a political motive but I said nothing.

"I can't think of anything else at the moment," he said. "But whatever the motive, it's a murder without clues."

I wagged my finger at him. "Didn't you say that it's only a murder without clues according to the Turkish police?"

Miss Wolff let out a ringing laugh.

"Are you saying that if Miss Marple were here, she'd solve it?" she said.

Otto had understood what I meant. He pursed his lips.

"I'm thinking," said Miss Bauer, "and I think you're right. The only person to gain from this murder has been me."

"Don't be silly, Annette," said Gust. Then, looking me straight in the eyes to reassure me that he was telling the truth, he said, "We were together on the night of the murder. Annette never left my side."

That wasn't news to me; nevertheless it was worth sacrificing an evening, just to hear them both admit it in front of everyone.

Gust must have felt he needed to explain the situation to the others. "I'm going to divorce my wife. Annette and I love each other," he said. Miss Wolff smiled sympathetically.

Gust was now holding Miss Bauer's hand tightly. He gave me a sidelong glance. "The night Kurt was killed, it was dawn before…" Before finishing his sentence, he pushed aside Miss Bauer's red hair and placed a kiss on her earlobe. "We were together all night. Annette didn't leave my side for a moment."

"I'm sorry, Miss Marple," said Miss Bauer, raising her glass to me.

8

I woke up to the telephone and to Lale telling me she couldn't take me to the airport because she simply had to get to the office. This meant I had to find a taxi at the crack of dawn, but I was glad Lale had gone off to work at her usual early hour.

I got myself ready without too many distractions, locked the balcony doors, checked the windows a hundred times and called the landlady on the top floor to say I would be away for ten days. It was almost eleven o'clock when I left home. I'm not really someone who believes in arriving at the airport two hours before a flight; the only reason for leaving so early that morning was to make sure I really had a ticket.

When I asked the taxi driver to take me to the airport, there was no "Can you direct me there, miss?", no wailing Turkish arabesque music, and no excuse about having to overcharge me because he didn't have change.

At the Turkish Airlines desk, everything was in order. Three minutes after giving them my name, I had a ticket in my hand.

In short, I was having a lucky day.

I didn't waste any time gazing round the duty-free shops, but went straight to gate eleven to board the flight, which was announced to be leaving shortly.

The plane was full. The moment I boarded, I felt the heaviness of the air on my face. In Istanbul, the only place I ever see such a dowdy lot of people is at the airport when boarding a plane to Berlin. Yes, the culture shock had started already.

It was difficult to get to my seat because of migrant workers pushing their badly packed bags and sacks into place. I sat down next to a fat, elderly woman wearing a headscarf, who was clearly searching avidly for some victim with whom to engage in trivial conversation. I immediately took out a book and started reading. The woman made her first attempt at conversation before I had even finished the first sentence. I responded by pretending to be a non-Turkish-speaking German tourist, which is what I always do on flights to Berlin if things are too bad.

"Do you live in Berlin?" asked the elderly woman, tucking in the corner of her headscarf.

"*Ich spreche leider kein Türkisch*," I said with a smile.

"*Ach, so!*" said the woman and she turned hopefully to a German tourist wearing shorts, who was sitting on her other side.

Without the slightest twinge of conscience, I went back to my book. This time, I'd just reached the end of the first sentence when I found one of the hostesses at my side and speaking to me. In German.

"Excuse me, I wonder if you would mind changing seats?" she said.

"Why? Am I sitting in the wrong seat?" I asked, trying to find my boarding pass in the pocket of the seat in front.

"No, no, you're in the right seat," said the hostess, whose heavy make-up made her look like a painted doll.

"Then why?" I asked.

"They've put a gentleman next to two women at the front, and these women say they won't sit next to a man. There aren't any empty seats on the plane so I wondered if you would change places with the gentleman."

I pointed to the woman sitting next to me and said, "Don't ask me, ask her. Then everyone will be happy."

The hostess looked vexed, turned to my neighbour and said the same thing in Turkish. The headscarved woman didn't wait to be asked twice. She got out of her seat with some difficulty, but with obvious pleasure at escaping her non-Turkish-speaking travel companions. As she walked towards the front, I sat up straight, trying to see the sex pervert who was coming to sit next to me.

All those people who, a short while ago, had been in the aisle shoving and pushing their bags into the overhead luggage storage were now seated. Apart from the headscarved woman waddling to her new seat, the only person standing was a tall, grey-haired man, who was talking to the hostesses. I sat up straight in order to have a good look at him.

Oh my God, what a vision!

"It can't be that man," I thought. What sane woman would not want to sit next to him? And what's more, thigh to thigh?

The man, one of God's gifts to women, thanked the hostesses and made his way towards the seat next to me.

"Don't get your hopes up," I said to myself. "He's probably going to the bathroom."

He stopped by my seat and said in German, "I'm afraid I have to disturb you."

I got up to make way for him. After we had both settled in our seats, I watched him out of the corner of my eye as he fastened his seatbelt, took a thick book and some newspapers out of his bag and put them in the pocket in front of him. I wasn't sure how to set about starting up a conversation with him. I searched for a line that would show, before take-off, what a brilliant and nice person I was. In the end, I pointed to the roll of newspapers in his hand and asked, "Could I have a look at your *Günebakan?*"

He looked startled, turned towards me and said, "Unfortunately, I didn't buy the *Günebakan*. But the hostesses will bring the papers round soon."

The man sitting by the window leaned forwards to have a look at me. I wondered if he'd heard me say "I don't know Turkish" to the headscarved woman. But I didn't care.

"Do you live in Berlin?" I asked, inspired by thoughts of the headscarved woman.

"No, I live in Istanbul." He clearly wasn't the talkative type. However, once I was set on something, I wasn't the sort to give up whatever the cost. And this was the case now.

"I live in Istanbul too," I said. He nodded. "There was some problem about the seating, I believe," I added.

"You realize what happened," he said.

"The hostess asked if I'd change places with you," I said.

"It's the first time anything like that has happened to me," he said. He seemed to be still in shock. "I normally travel business class, but this time I had to book at the last minute and that was the only remaining seat. The scene at the airport was bad enough, but this…" He shook his head in disbelief. "For someone to call a hostess and say, 'We won't sit next to this man', it's almost as if they had something personal against me…"

"Oh no," I said. "Actually it didn't seem strange to me. If you can't sit next to women on intercity buses, why shouldn't the same apply to aeroplanes?"

He laughed.

"I think you've been living in Turkey for a long time."

"Long enough," I said.

"I've no objection to women sitting next to each other, but…"

He was taking this far too seriously.

I interrupted him, saying, "I don't think you should worry about it." I just managed to stop myself from adding, "I'm sure there are lots of women who would give their life to sit next to you."

We developed our acquaintance further as the aeroplane began its descent over Berlin. He was a lawyer who handled international trade lawsuits and, as far as I could understand from his answers to my indirect questioning, he was a bachelor and did not even have a girlfriend. That he was a lawyer was understandable, but I simply could not comprehend how he could still be a bachelor. It seemed that Lale's theory, which I had been trying to disprove for years, that all attractive men in Istanbul are either married or gay, was about to be proved groundless. I have a feeling that you're wondering how I could be so certain that Selim, this man I'd been sitting next to for three hours, wasn't gay. Well, as Miss Wolff had said the previous night, I now say, "It was a hunch, and you have to trust me." Is that enough for you? There may be readers who protest that my hunches are not to be trusted when it comes to solving murder cases. To them, my reply is simply that everyone has some area of expertise and, at that time, mine was not in catching murderers.

Selim was going to the Hilton Hotel in Gendarmenmarkt, an area that was once on the East Berlin border and which, after the Berlin Wall came down, attracted a lot of investment and became a place where yuppies went to enjoy themselves.

We walked towards the line of taxis in front of Tegel Airport, that ugly sprawl beyond the outer suburbs of the city. Selim said, "I'll drop you off first and then go to my hotel."

"I'm going straight to the hospital," I said.

"What will you do with your suitcase?"

I've never been able to travel light so I was used to my luggage being a problem.

"I'll take it with me to the hospital," I said.

We'd reached the front of the taxi queue. Seeing our luggage, the taxi driver ran round to open up the car boot.

"Where are you going to stay?" asked Selim.

"I'll stay at my mother's house, but I have to get the key and I want to speak to my mother's doctors as soon as possible. So, I must go to the hospital first," I said.

The driver quickly loaded up the car boot and got into the driving seat.

"First to Urban Hospital, and then on to somewhere else," I said.

"I could take your suitcase to my hotel and you could come and collect it when you're finished," said Selim.

I coughed as if I had something stuck in my throat.

"Is it far from the hospital to the hotel?"

"No," I said. Any woman of my age who doesn't have a lover learns to read the signs of male behaviour. Selim had just made two proposals within five minutes, from which I inferred that his interest in me was at least equal to my interest in him. Men, unlike women, never act completely altruistically. They always have an agenda. That meant there were two possibilities. Either Selim was taking my suitcase and me from place to place because he fancied me, or he was sticking to me because he didn't know the city well and didn't want to be there on his own.

I decided to ignore my negative thoughts for now and enjoy the moment. In any case, I had to put these thoughts aside and concentrate on my mother lying in hospital.

"Fractures mend slowly in old people," said my mother. She had placed her purple-veined hands, which seemed smaller every time I saw her, side by side on the white hospital bedcover.

"It's time you had a manicure," I said, touching her left hand and wanting to change the subject. We had been talking about illnesses and hospitals continuously for about an hour.

"Phh," she said.

Ever since she'd been too unwell to go to the hairdresser, that is for the last four years, a woman had been coming once a fortnight to give her a manicure, and once a month to dye her hair.

"I can't be bothered with manicures any more," she said, but she didn't take her eyes off her hands.

I resolved to send a manicurist to the hospital the very next day.

"I don't want that sort of thing here," she said, as if reading my thoughts. "I mean it," she added. "If you really want to do something, bring me a proper cup of coffee tomorrow. What they give us here is like dishwater. Why have I been paying for private health insurance all these years if I can't get a decent cup of coffee? I have a room to myself, that's all. I suppose I have to be grateful for that. If I'd been in a two-bed room with a Turk lying next to me, you'd have had to take me out in a coffin. Sometimes it's difficult to tell whether this is a hospital or a picnic spot. All you need is one of them staying in hospital for a hundred visitors to turn up. And…" – she straightened up slightly, indicating that she wanted me to rearrange her pillows – "and they don't know German. I said to the Turkish nurse, 'The Turks in Turkey speak better German than you do.' She didn't react at all. Phh. So much for integration. And now, they're using our money to set up integration courses for the Turks. To be paid for by Mrs Hirschel." She put her hand on her heart.

She pointed to the shelves by her bedside. "Give me that newspaper." She turned over the pages and waved the paper in front of my face. "Look, read this."

"I'll get a paper on my way out, Mother. I'm going to go and talk to your doctor. You need to calm down, otherwise your blood pressure will go up."

"Oh yes, up goes my blood pressure. I mustn't get worked up," she said. I kissed her on her dimples, now lost among the brownish marks on her face. "I'm going," I said.

"First call that Turkish nurse for me."

"Tell me what you want."

"No, call the nurse."

I left as the nurse came through the door.

Ignoring the taxis that were waiting outside the hospital, I walked for a while in order to clear my head. The duty doctor had said my mother could be discharged from hospital whenever I wanted. The only problem was finding a care home for her.

"There are some excellent care homes that I can recommend," the doctor had said. However, first I had to persuade my mother to stay in a care home, and this didn't seem at all possible to me.

I continued walking quickly. I was talking to myself, trying to find words that would sound reasonable to my mother. "You'd be better looked after there, Mother, and you'd have lots of friends," I was saying. "It's difficult for old people to live in big cities... We could find a care home wherever you wanted. There's even a place in Mallorca where Germans stay. And the people who work there are German. Or there's the Black Forest..."

When I arrived in front of Selim's hotel it was still twilight. I went through the revolving door, approached the friendliest-looking of the girls at reception and smiled. I was about to open my mouth when I realized I didn't know Selim's surname.

"Can I help you?" said the receptionist, looking at my still-open mouth.

"I was supposed to be meeting someone who's staying at your hotel, but I don't know his surname," I said. "He's Turkish and he arrived earlier this evening. His name is Selim." I blushed uncomfortably.

"Actually, we're not allowed to give out the numbers of our clients' rooms, but…" She looked around and said, "Just for once, I'll make an exception." She laughed. "How do you write the name?" I spelt out the name for her. The girl gazed at the computer in front of her and said nothing for a while. I listened to the rapid clatter of her fingers on the keyboard.

"I've found it. Öztürk," she said, and the clattering stopped. "That's probably a Turkish surname, isn't it?"

Smiling, I nodded in agreement.

"Room 532. You can telephone from here."

She dialled through on the telephone in front of her and handed me the receiver.

"I'll be down right away. Let's go out and eat," said Selim, as soon as he heard my voice.

Actually, what I really wanted was to take a shower and stretch out in front of a B-grade film, rather than go out for dinner. The last thing I wanted was to have to drag my suitcase over to my mother's house. I sat down to wait in one of the lobby armchairs where I could see the lift.

Selim came out of the lift after a couple of minutes. My stomach lurched, he was so handsome. Still sitting in the chair, I studied his physique as he walked towards me, and his face as he stood next to me. He bent towards me and took my hand to help me to my feet. He wasn't much taller than me. I looked into his eyes… His eyes were different shades of green with flecks of brown. He held my hand between his palms, pulled me towards him and pressed his cheek against mine. His cheek was smooth and without a trace of aftershave. I breathed in his human smell, his masculine smell. I refrained from whispering in his ear, "Forget dinner, let's go upstairs."

"Where are we going to eat?" I asked.

"There's a good kebab place nearby," he said. His face was serious.

Just then, I understood why I hated Germans who always drink beer and Turks who always eat kebabs.

"Or do you want to take your suitcase and get back to your mother's house?" he said. He was looking at me teasingly.

"I thought lawyers didn't make jokes," I said.

"It's not good to have prejudices," he said. I laughed. In the distance, the girl at reception raised her head and looked over at me.

We were still standing in the lobby holding hands. I took my hand away and picked my bag up from the chair. As he walked ahead to open the door for me, I took a good look at his backside. Not bad at all. Especially for his age.

We walked for a while in silence. When we reached the German Cathedral, I again asked, "Where are we going?"

"Here," he said, pointing to a place just ahead of us. "It's a place called Borchardt, nothing amazing. I find it an interesting place not because of the food but because you can find yourself eating next to a German government minister at a restaurant which is cheap even by Istanbul standards. The last time I came here, a minister was sitting at the table right next to us. She didn't even have a bodyguard."

I felt an urge to reach out and stroke his hair. Do good Turks like this really deserve those Turkish politicians, for God's sake?

Borchardt was quiet, as I expected on a Sunday evening. Nevertheless, they sat us at one of the tables near the door, in case any of their regular clients happened to turn up, even at that time.

Selim sat down, and immediately spread his napkin over his knees.

"I really wanted to drink something before we ate, but I'm very hungry. Have an aperitif if you like," he said.

"No, I'll have a glass of wine with you."

The waiter threw some menus on the table and dashed off.

"The service here is totally unreasonable. They wouldn't let men like that be waiters anywhere except Germany," Selim said, watching the waiter move away.

"The waiters at this restaurant are probably professionals, but those who work in the cafés are all university students. That's why the service is bad," I said.

"Fine, but it doesn't matter to customers who's doing the work. Whether it's a student or a bricklayer, I want good service."

"You're right," I said.

We both ordered schnitzels, and red wine.

He ordered in German, and very good German it was too.

"Where did you learn German?" I asked, as soon as the waiter went away.

"I studied in Switzerland," he said.

"What did you study?"

"Law, of course."

"Of course," I said.

"You don't like lawyers very much," he said.

"Actually, I wouldn't say I don't like them," I said. "Anyway, my father was a lawyer."

"You said your family lived in Turkey when you were a child, didn't you? Was it because of your father's work?"

"Not really. He and my mother escaped from the war, or rather Fascism. My father was Jewish, a law professor. We lived in Istanbul until 1965, and then returned to Germany. If it had been up to my father, we'd have stayed, but my mother wanted to come back. My brother and I were both born in Istanbul."

"So, when did you return to Istanbul?"

"In '88. My decision to settle in Istanbul is a long story. I went there for a week to visit a friend, and I've been there for thirteen years."

"OK, but didn't you have problems getting a residency permit or work permit?"

"Ah, you lawyers! What strange things you ask about," I said.

He shrugged his shoulders.

"My father took Turkish citizenship in the 1950s. He was one of the few refugees in Turkey to do so at that time, and he kept it until he died. As you know, if the father or mother is Turkish, then the children are too."

He nodded thoughtfully. He looked upset.

"What's the matter?" I asked.

"I was thinking how memories of the war still remain fresh."

"It's only fifty years... Of course they're fresh. Just think, some survivors of the concentration camps are still living. I sometimes find it difficult to believe that there was such deep suffering in our recent history."

"Yes," he said. "Yes. It was so..." He couldn't find the words.

Just then, the waiter put a plate in front of me that was almost completely covered with an enormous schnitzel. From the first mouthful, I realized that, despite its size, I would have no difficulty eating the whole thing.

"How do you feel about yourself?"

"What do you mean, how do I feel?"

"Which culture do you feel closest to?"

"I'm an *İstanbullu*," I said. "The only place in the world where I feel at home is Istanbul. Maybe that's because Istanbul is the only place that has no objection to me being myself… After a while, people don't distinguish between which experiences they have selected for themselves and which have been dished out to them. I have a *bona fide* Turkish passport, yet in Turkey I'm a German. A German who speaks good Turkish. And when I'm in Germany, despite having a German passport and the fact that my mother's a Roman Catholic, I'm a Jew."

After dinner, we returned to the hotel where the girl at reception was still sitting where we'd left her. She smiled at us.

"Do you want to come up, or shall I bring your suitcase downstairs?" asked Selim.

"If you don't mind fetching it, I won't come up," I said. "I'm so tired I'm ready to drop."

He hurried towards the lift, turned and called out, "I'll be right back." To pass the time, I looked at the shop-window displays in the lobby. What strange things they were selling.

"Come on," he whispered in my ear, making me jump. He was holding my suitcase and standing right behind me.

I reached out to take the suitcase. "Let me take you," he said.

"Whatever next?" I said.

"I'm going to take you home," he said and strode towards the door. I ran after him.

"Don't be ridiculous, I'll get a taxi home," I said.

"You're German," he said laughing. "You'd go and take the metro, just because it's cheap. Unless I saw it with my own eyes, I'd never believe you went by taxi." As he opened the door for me to pass, he was still laughing.

Apart from telling the driver the address, we didn't speak again until the taxi stopped outside my mother's house.

"Shall I call you at the hotel tomorrow afternoon?" I asked before getting out of the taxi.

"I have a very busy schedule tomorrow and I don't know what time I'll be back at the hotel," he said.

I turned my head away so that he wouldn't see I was upset, opened the door and jumped out. He got out behind me. I felt certain my face had turned bright red. I kept my eyes fixed to the ground.

He held my hand, or rather the tips of my fingers and, as if explaining to a small child why the seasons change, said, "We don't need to telephone each other. Let's meet tomorrow evening at eight o'clock," he said. "There's a Thai restaurant I like very much. It's in the East, in Prenzlauer Allee. Let's go there to eat." Without letting go of my hand, he patted his jacket pocket with his other hand looking for pen and paper.

"Here," I said, taking a small notebook out of my bag. He placed it on top of the taxi and wrote down the address.

"Do you know it from memory?"

"It's my favourite restaurant, of course I do."

I put the diary back in my bag and offered him my cheek.

"Just a minute, let me take your suitcase up the steps," he said.

"You're going too far now," I said.

He put his head through the window and asked the driver, who was sitting motionlessly in his seat, to open the car boot.

9

When I woke up the next morning, I was surprised to find that I wasn't feeling like the happiest woman in the world. One aspect of ageing I didn't like was my increasing sense of duty. It prevented me from forgetting my responsibilities and devoting myself wholeheartedly to the business of love.

As I went into the shower, my mind was not on Selim, but on my mother. This was very sad for a forty-three-year-old woman. The water was still dripping down my legs when I rang my brother Schalom.

It was Ute who answered. "Are you in Berlin?" she asked. "Yes," I said. "We need to get Mother out of hospital and find a suitable place to care for her."

"Wait, I'll call Schalom," she said.

After putting the phone down, I dressed and went out for breakfast. I walked along the side of the canal, reading the menus posted on the doors of the row of cafés. My mother's house was in the Turkish district of Kreuzberg, known as "little Istanbul" by Germans who keep away from Turks and this area. Anyone who has seen a single postcard of Istanbul would never refer to this miserable place as "little Istanbul", but never mind.

Because this area used to have the Berlin Wall next to it, the German working classes didn't want to settle in Kreuzberg. Therefore while the Wall existed, rents hit rock bottom and the Turks who came as *Gastarbeiter* after 1965 settled in Kreuzberg because it was cheap. First it was these workers and then, during my student years, it was left-wing Germans… Non-Turkish guest-workers gradually left Germany as the economies of their own countries improved. It meant that, during those years, the only new arrivals were Turks, who married, had lots of children and continued to live in Kreuzberg.

I've never worked out why my parents chose to live in that area, which I associated so much with migrants. I could understand my father wanting to live there when we returned from Istanbul, but my mother continued living in that house even after he died, despite all her complaints about Turks. My mother liked to confuse people around her by speaking in Turkish. Even so, it was ridiculous to think that she'd lived there all those years just to hear a headscarved young cashier say, "*Teyze*, where did you learn your Turkish?" a couple of times a week at one of the Turkish markets in Kreuzberg. Also, she used to say that if anyone called her "*teyze*", meaning "auntie", it made her so cross she wanted to hurl the olives, or whatever she had bought, back at them.

Sometimes I used to think the reason why my mother didn't move away from Kreuzberg was that she loved water. Although originally from Munich, my mother had spent her childhood in Hamburg. Unlike my father, who was from Trier, she had always lived near the sea. My mother found Istanbul too Muslim and never really liked it, so I think the reason she agreed to remain there after the war was her love of water. The only water visible in Berlin, if you don't count the lakes nearby, is in the canals that wind around the city and the River Spree. My mother loved her house by the canal, even if she didn't love Kreuzberg.

On my last visit, she'd said that sometimes she thought the canal smelled like the Bosphorus.

But she became annoyed when I said, "I think you're missing Istanbul."

I decided to head for some cafés with a view of the light railway that I'd discovered on one of my visits to Berlin. However, having studied all the menus on the café doors in Paul-Lincke-Ufer, I waited in vain for a waiter to run up to me saying, "This way, madam, we have crunchy *simit*, honey, cream and a host of olives." I realized I'd been wasting my time.

Leaving the canal behind me, I turned into Manteuffel Street. I liked both the view and the breakfast at Café Morgenland, which was right on the corner of the street next to Görlitzer metro station, referred to as Gülizar station by Turks.

What I really wanted was the Italian salami breakfast but, thinking of mad cow disease, I just ordered cheese.

While waiting for my breakfast to arrive, I took out my notebook and wrote a list of arguments I'd been storing in my head since the previous day for persuading my mother to go into a care home.

That afternoon, I entered the hospital room with a thermos of coffee in my hands, feeling like a child who has done her homework properly.

*

Later, as I waited in the queue outside the Thai restaurant in Prenzlauer Allee, I lit a cigarette and exhaled, feeling pleased with myself.

The moment I'd mentioned the words care home, my mother had said, "I've been thinking of that for a long time. In any case, I don't have many friends left in Berlin. Those that haven't died have moved into care homes." As if to convince herself, she'd added, "I think that would be the best thing to do."

I was amazed. Perhaps because, for some reason, I'd had the belief that no elderly person, especially a woman like my mother, would ever want to go into a care home. My brother was right. I'd started to think like a Turk about some things, though not everything of course. I'd come to believe that it was a disaster for anyone to go into a care home. Yet in Germany, care homes are a part of life; there's a place to suit everyone.

When I left the hospital, I'd gone into a nearby café and drunk two glasses of sparkling wine, to celebrate the fact that, for the first time in her life, my mother had acted like a "normal" woman. From there I went to my favourite bookshop in Oranien Street. Then I'd gone home, put my feet up and even read for a while before getting ready to go out in the evening. Now, I was standing in a queue outside the restaurant where I'd arranged to meet Selim.

"You're miles away," said a voice. Selim. He was carrying an enormous briefcase and wearing a beige linen suit with his tie undone.

"Hi," I said, in a chirpy voice that sounded alien even to my ears.

He bowed his head in response and gestured towards a man in a suit standing right behind him.

"Let me introduce you. Jean… Kati…" He didn't say our surnames. I shook hands with the man.

"Do you speak French?" he asked me.

"Not very well," I replied.

"In that case," he said, looking at Jean, "let's speak in German."

We had now reached the front of the queue and were led to a table for four near the kitchen.

As Selim studied the menu, he gave his friend a most important piece of information about me.

"Kati doesn't really like lawyers. In fact her father was a lawyer, but…"

"Really? What's your father's name? We might know him," Jean interrupted eagerly.

"Abraham Hirschel," I said. Jean looked as if he couldn't believe his ears. "You mean the criminal lawyer Abraham Hirschel was your father?" he cried.

"Yes," I said. I was used to people reacting when they heard my father's name mentioned; I had even learned to enjoy their amazement.

"Your father was a genius in criminal law."

"That's what they say," I said proudly. "You must be a criminal lawyer too, I think."

He nodded.

"Don't you know of my father?" I asked Selim, who was sitting opposite me.

"Yes, I do, or rather I know his name. He was involved with Turkish… But criminal law has little in common with what I do."

"Selim spends most of his time in the committee meetings of faceless companies," said Jean teasingly.

The Thai waiter planted himself next to our table, notepad in hand.

"I'm going to drink beer. And I suggest you don't drink the wine," said Selim.

Jean and I both ordered beer.

"The food here is very good, but as you see…" he indicated the interior of the restaurant. "It's not a place to drink wine. It's really a peasant restaurant," he whispered.

"Tell me what to eat," I said.

"If you like fish, number seventy-nine is very good. It's dried fish. The Thais cook it with vegetables. But if you can't take spicy food, have something else."

"I like spicy," I said. "I'll order number seventy-nine."

Selim and Jean ordered steamed trout with celeriac.

Jean got up to go and wash his hands before the meal and Selim leaned across the table towards me.

"I'm sorry," he said. "I would have preferred it if we'd been alone, but Jean has to go back to Brussels tomorrow and tonight is the only time we had to see each other. I had to bring him along."

"No problem," I said with understanding, like a woman of experience. Selim stroked my hand lightly with his forefinger as silent recognition of my generous attitude.

Jean removed his jacket with newly washed hands and hung it over the back of his chair. "It's a bit strange for someone who lives in Istanbul to know Berlin restaurants better than you do, isn't it?" he said. Selim had obviously not told him much about me.

"I also live in Istanbul," I explained.

"The last I heard, your father was in Berlin."

"Yes, but I went back to Istanbul."

He lifted one eyebrow. "Are you happy there?"

"Very much so. It's been thirteen years."

He nodded his head pensively.

"Ah!" he said, raising his hand as if he had just thought of something. "I asked Selim about something on the way here in the taxi but he couldn't tell me. Since you live in Istanbul, maybe you know something about it. This murder case... I read about it in the paper..."

My heart began to pound.

"Which murder?" I interrupted. "You mean the Müller murder?" The words tumbled out of my mouth.

"See," he said, turning to Selim. "Those who read the papers know about it."

"Well, it's something that comes into Kati's area of interest," said Selim.

"What do you mean, her area of interest?"

"Kati sells crime fiction. She has the only shop in Istanbul that sells detective stories."

Turning to Jean, I intervened. "What were you going to ask?"

"I was going to ask what happened. Have they found the murderer?"

"No, he wasn't found and probably never will be. There was an interview with the inspector dealing with the case in yesterday's *Westdeutsche Zeitung*. As far as I understand, the police don't have a single lead, so yet another murder case will be closed and remain unsolved." As I said this, I realized how upset I felt that my first venture into detective work had ended unsuccessfully.

"It's interesting that the German police didn't ask to be brought into the investigation," said Jean, lighting a cigarette.

"How do you know they didn't want to?"

"If they had, they would have done so."

"As far as I know, their request was denied."

To be certain what I meant, he asked again.

"You mean they wanted to be involved and their request was denied? That's very interesting; are you sure?"

"Why is it interesting?"

He scratched his ear, deep in thought. "If the police in the country of a murder victim want to be involved in an investigation that is being carried out in the country where the murder took place, that request is generally not denied. Especially between countries such as Turkey and Germany which have such strong judicial ties... I wonder why they said no?" The last sentence seemed to be addressed to himself.

Selim laughed.

"My dear friends, there's no need to think too long about it. If you knew the slightest thing about Turks, you would know that it was not at all surprising."

"How do you mean?" said Jean. He was still scratching his ear.

Selim pursed his lips. "Haven't you heard of something called national sovereignty?" he asked. He pointed to me. "You know what national sovereignty means to us."

"Say it in a way that I can understand too," pleaded Jean.

"Turkish police would never accept the aid of foreign police to solve a murder that took place within their area of jurisdiction. They won't accept help from outside even if it means the murder remains unsolved. No one is allowed to interfere with the internal workings of the Turkish state. And in the case of police work, even the government can't interfere."

I rolled my eyes. "That's all well and good, but the police say there's no evidence," I said. "That means there were no fingerprints, no witness statements, no blood traces and not even a button or a strand of hair was left at the murder scene. Most importantly, nobody had a motive for killing him. So tell me, how are they to get to the bottom of such a murder? Would German police find evidence the Turkish police couldn't?"

"Why not?" said Jean, shrugging his shoulders.

"Why not?" I exclaimed. "You talk as if you don't know how inept the German police are. Don't you remember the attempted bank robbery when two girls were taken hostage? The police killed one of the hostages instead of the robbers."

"You're right. They're hopeless at hostage situations. But the German police are good at solving murders. And of course there's the question of technology; quite simply, the Germans have better equipment."

"Well, that's a great example of prejudice," I said. "Solving a murder has nothing to do with technology. Murders are solved with the mind." I continued talking, my voice rising like that of a primary-school teacher.

"The skill of a country's police at catching suspects is not proportionate to its national per capita income. The same goes for health. Everyone thinks that because Turkey is poor, the health service must be bad. But when it comes to diagnosis, Turkish doctors are far better than German doctors."

"Fine, but you're citing an example where Germans perform really badly. It's no secret that the health service is falling apart in Germany. And yes, the doctors are particularly bad at diagnosis. But unravelling a murder is something else. Even…" Jean scratched his ear while he thought, and then said, "I don't remember the exact figures, but statistically the proportion of murders solved by German police is very high."

"Whatever," I said, "I'm not really interested in this good cop/bad cop debate. Why does this murder interest you?"

He fixed his gaze pensively on a point above my head and said, "I've been trying to nail Müller for two years."

I was startled. Who would have thought that I would learn the secret about Müller in this ordinary little Thai restaurant?

"Why?" I asked, trying to maintain my composure. The waiter brought us a huge plate of rice and Jean waited for him to move away.

"I don't know if you remember," he said. "At the end of the eighties, there was a series of child murders that rocked Western Europe. Actually, child massacre would be more accurate. Twelve bodies of children between the ages of four and nine were found one after the other. The abducted children were first raped and then killed…"

"Stop," I almost screamed. I closed my mouth and ran to the bathroom. For the first time since childhood my intestines had lost all control.

"This…" I thought, with my head in the toilet bowl, "This is all because of what happened to Petra's son Peter…" I'd wanted to throw up then when I'd first heard about it but couldn't.

I had long since digested the cheese I'd eaten at breakfast, and nothing else had entered my stomach apart from the coffee I'd drunk at the hospital with my mother and two glasses of sparkling wine. At that moment, as I held my head inside the toilet bowl and felt my knees, which I tended so carefully with expensive

221

lotions, bear down on the tiled bathroom floor of this cheap restaurant, I was glad I hadn't eaten much.

Once I was finished, I closed the toilet lid and sat on it. I stayed there like that for perhaps five minutes while I prepared myself to face the outside world. I rose and saw my face in the mirror above the washbasin. I looked frightful, as if I'd been crying, but at least my make-up hadn't run. I dampened a paper towel under the tap and wiped my cheeks. As I came out of the door, over which there was a picture of a child sitting on a potty, I came face to face with Selim, who was leaning against a cigarette vending machine and waiting for me. He studied my face anxiously.

"What happened?"

"It was something I ate at lunch, I think," I said, lowering my head, not because I was lying, but because the way he was looking at me had made me feel uncomfortable. I walked briskly back to the table and sat down heavily on the chair that Selim politely pulled out for me. The number seventy-nine fish that I'd ordered with such relish was on the table in front of me. I pushed the plate as far away from me as possible.

"I can't eat this," I said to Selim apologetically. "Would you order me some jasmine tea?"

"Are you all right?" asked Jean.

Trying to smile, I said, "I've been working very hard recently." It wasn't a lie. "You were telling us why you were after Müller."

"Let's forget about those nasty subjects. Why don't we talk about Turkish politics?" suggested Selim, as he stopped my hand from reaching out for the cigarette packet. "Perhaps it's better not to smoke just now," he said tenderly.

I didn't need a mirror to guess the awful expression on my face. Selim immediately retracted.

"OK, smoke if you want to. I was just thinking of you."

Jean was clearly not too happy to be witnessing a power struggle between two people in the process of flirting with each other. He was keener than I was to return to the matter of Müller. He watched Selim light my cigarette and carried on talking.

"The police failed to find out what happened to the abducted children. Within seven months, twelve children were abducted, one after the other. The bodies were found some time after the abductions. The police followed up a few leads but nothing came of them."

"Where did the children come from? I mean, which country did this happen in?" I asked, fearing the answer I would get.

"The first child was abducted in West Germany and the body was found in a wooded area between Brussels and Bruges. The second child was from Belgium, and children were also abducted in Holland and France. Their bodies were found two or three weeks later. They were found in different places, sometimes by a motorway, sometimes in a wood... Everything was too professional to have been carried out by a simple pervert. It was a long time before they discovered any clues about the abductions or where the children had been taken. There was a witness statement giving a description of a suspect for one abduction case, but it bore no resemblance to the suspect in the next case. It was obviously a paedophile ring, rather than a single pervert."

"You said before that a few clues were found."

"Yes, a tip-off led police to the house where the children were taken." He popped some strange pink vegetable that was lying on his plate into his mouth and continued speaking. "So they found the house, but it contained no clues that could lead them any further. In fact…"

"Yeah?" I said.

"It was established that the children were used for making porn movies. The basement was found to be kitted out as a studio."

"Fingerprints, blood traces?…"

"No, the place had been thoroughly cleaned before the police got there. That was surprising of course, because one had to ask why didn't they just burn the place down. But it was not the only strange thing about this case, which was the most complex and intractable case I've ever known."

"What happened two years ago?" I asked.

"What do you mean, two years ago? Hah, yes, because I said I'd been after Müller for two years… The police were tipped off about some child porn which they'd then seized from a video shop selling sex films in Paris. These films are generally made in the Far East or Russia, but one of the films caught their attention."

I interrupted him.

"Are the police still looking for the murderers of those twelve children?"

"Well, the file isn't closed of course. But the reason this film drew attention was its technological features and high-quality backdrops; it had nothing to do with what happened all those years ago when those children were undoubtedly used for pornographic films."

I screwed up my face with revulsion.

"Yes, you're right," said Jean. Selim was sitting in silence.

"It's detestable, but that's how it is. The film techniques used in child porn are generally very crude. That sort of film is usually made by a single pervert using amateur camera equipment. But this film had been made with superior lighting and equipment. That's what drew the attention of the police."

"Shall we close this subject?" said Selim.

"Just a minute," I said. "Can't you explain without going into so much detail?"

"I don't exactly enjoy talking about this filth," said Jean.

"What happened in the end? I mean, how did you get on to Müller?"

"When it was proved that the child in the film found at the porn shop in Clichy was Wim, a child abducted from a children's home in Rotterdam who, like the other kids, was then killed, the porn seller was interrogated about how he came by the film. I'm cutting this short because you asked me to. Anyway, it finally emerged that Müller was in that gang and was the person who had actually made the films. That came to light when another paedophile admitted under interrogation that he'd been used to help with the child abductions. He'd hoped to get a reduced sentence by telling what he knew about the ring. That man referred to Müller by name in a statement he made shortly before he was killed."

"Before he was killed?"

"His body was found in the prison shower before he could make a statement in court."

"Was that gang really so powerful?" I asked. My stomach had begun to churn again.

"Yeah," he said, "I think it was a very big operation."

"So, do you think it was that gang that murdered Müller?"

"Definitely, to stop him making a statement."

"But the way the murder was carried out... Isn't that a bit strange?"

I was curious to see how much more he could come up with.

"Wasn't the murder carried out with a hair-dryer?" he said.

I nodded.

"Yes, well. What killer would carry out a murder like that? It looked very amateurish, except that no clues were left behind, so in that respect it could have been a professional job. However, if the gang had hired a killer, he would have..."

"Would have used a gun," I said, completing his sentence. He suddenly stopped and pondered what I had said. "I think it's all very dirty and very complex," he said with distaste.

"Are you the lawyer for one of the children's families?"

"Hah, well, that's an important point. The gang selected the children carefully; they didn't leave anything to chance. Of the twelve children, five were orphans living in children's homes. The others were from children of deprived families or refugees, families that had neither the financial means nor the social standing to deal with this."

"In that case, who engaged you?" I asked.

"I'm representing a Cameroonian family that was granted asylum in Belgium. A friend of mine who knows that I specialize in crimes against children suggested that the family should speak to me. Once I'd studied the case a bit, I took it on without payment. But in ten years, we've got nowhere. Just when there's some hope of resolving it…" He sighed with irritation. "Well, as you see…"

"You mentioned a child abducted from West Germany," I said, keeping my face hidden behind my beer glass. "The first child to be abducted, did he also come from a children's home?"

It was as if events were repeating themselves. Why didn't he ask the reason for my interest in this particular child?

He put his head in his hands. "No. The child was being brought up by his elderly grandmother. His mother and father were living in Seoul. The mother was German and the father was Korean. They were the only ones out of all the families of these abducted children who could have done something about the situation, yet this couple showed little interest in the child or what followed. Nevertheless, I understand they employed a detective to get to the bottom of it all. But of course nothing came of it. The child was six or seven when he was killed."

"Do you remember his name?" I asked.

"Peter," he said sadly, almost sobbing. "How can you ask me if I remember? I know the names of each and every one of those children."

I lit another cigarette.

"That incident… Was the child living in a village on the Rhine?"

"If you can call it a village, yes. It had a strange name. Just a minute…" He gestured with his hand to stop us interrupting him or his thoughts.

"Pfaffenheck!" he said. "Yes, yes, it was Pfaffenheck. The mother's name was Gudrun Kim. While working on that file, I learned that over half of all Koreans are called Kim."

"You mean that the child was half-oriental and half-German," I said.

"Yes," he said. "But if you ask me, he didn't have the physical appearance of an oriental." He shrugged his shoulders and scratched his ear at the same time. "It's of no interest to me what people get up to in their married life."

"So that means Peter's mother's name was Gudrun," I said. I was saying out loud what was going through my mind. "So now what will happen?" I asked Jean.

"Nothing," he said. "Until Müller was killed, I'd hoped the murders could be solved. That man was the tip of the iceberg. According to the witness who made the statement to the police and later got killed, Müller set up the connections, which meant Müller undoubtedly knew the other members of the gang." He pursed his lips sadly, adding, "All those years of work for nothing."

"So had the case been closed?"

"Only a statement by Müller would have enabled us to go further. It might have meant we could get some more names. But now, there's nothing more to be done. As you see, I don't even keep up with the press articles about the Müller murder. It's over as far as I'm concerned." As he said that, he was scratching his ear again.

"I'm almost sad about Müller's murder," he said. He waved his hand behind his head as if wanting to indicate that these matters were now behind him.

"Yes," said Selim, slapping him on the back. "Let's talk about something positive."

For the remainder of the meal, I didn't open my mouth except to answer a question directed straight at me. There was no need for Selim to insist on taking me home that time. I was too tired and wrapped up in my thoughts to put up any kind of resistance.

When the taxi stopped outside my mother's house, my mind was on Petra and Peter so I didn't understand why Selim said, "I have to get up at seven o'clock tomorrow."

"You'll get up as long as you set the alarm," I said.

"What I mean is, I won't come up with you," he said. "Our first night should be special. We should at least be able to have breakfast together in the morning."

Perhaps it was his normality that brought me back to my normal self, I don't know. "Never mind that," I said. "If tonight is good, it means we'll have lots more mornings to have breakfast together."

The next morning, Selim really did get up at seven o'clock. After he left, I tossed and turned in bed, preparing numerous sentences in my head, but didn't like any of them. What was I going to say to Petra?

In fact, I didn't really say anything. Or rather, I said it all in a very brief telephone conversation.

"I now know who killed Müller."

"In that case, don't call me, call the police."

"I don't want to call the police."

"Why?"

"I think you've suffered enough. And I don't want you to go to jail. I just want you to know that I understand you."

I put the phone down and took my best outfit out of my suitcase. After all, I was going to visit my mother.

10

Three days later, while I was flying to Mallorca to settle my mother into a care home, Selim was returning to Istanbul to wrap up his business. By the time we met again in Berlin to go to Morocco together, I was going to need a good holiday, after spending a week with my mother in Mallorca.

People soon shrug off tiredness when they're in love, and I was as fresh as a new-born babe. Despite all the high-factor sun cream I used, I spent little time in the sun because I had no intention of developing premature wrinkles. Still, looking at my bikini line, I'd clearly developed quite a tan.

When we returned to Istanbul after three weeks away, it was clear that Pelin had really taken to the shop. Everything had gone like clockwork in my absence, proving that I wasn't essential, even if it was my shop.

Lale didn't resign from *Günebakan*, but was dismissed with compensation for her hard work and length of service. She's thinking of going to Cuba for a while and has no intention of going back to journalism when she comes back. God knows what she'll do.

There were some redundancies at Yılmaz's advertising company, but he succeeded in being one of the "essentials" who was kept on. I heard they'd reduced his salary, but he doesn't talk about that. The Istanbul stock market must be on the way up, because last Saturday it was he who ordered the teas at the café in Firuzağa.

And Fofo? He's still in love. In my absence, he took away his belongings and left his key with the landlord. Rude fellow, to treat me like that.

When I returned, I found a voicemail from Batuhan. I was terrified Selim would ask, "Who's that man?" You can never tell how these Turkish men will react.

I didn't call Petra again. And she didn't call me. A few days after our return from Morocco, Selim read out a news item over breakfast stating that the film crew was still in Istanbul. My new man is an avid reader of newspapers.

I guess Mesut will be in jail for a long time yet. When he comes out he'll have forgotten about me anyway. Still, it would be cool if he called to say he was sorry he couldn't make our date, wouldn't it?

Caterpillars and Another Thing

Selim has been in Adana for three days. On a business trip. One outcome of companies declaring bankruptcy and banks going under is that his secretary sees more of him than I do. The work of lawyers increases at times of crisis, because more people are unable to pay their debts and the number of thieves, bribe-takers, blackmailers and divorcees increases.

Don't think I'm complaining about Selim being away. Brief separations are good for a relationship and, to be honest, I'm rather good at amusing myself when I'm alone. However, for once, even the orange-coloured shiny patent-leather shoes that I bought recently in a sale didn't, and don't, bring a little smile to my face. There's something that keeps troubling me... Like a huge caterpillar that is gnawing away inside my brain.

You might ask what can be done about such irritations and I don't have a satisfactory answer. I have a good job, a lover I wouldn't be without, and friends with whom I can share my ups and downs. What more could a woman in early middle age want? OK, not quite so many wrinkles, a bit less cellulite perhaps. But I'm not the sort of woman to spend my time gazing at wrinkles and cellulite in this city of Istanbul where retaining one's beauty in later life has become an obsession.

…I'm not, whatever anyone says.

But why was I saying that? I realize you're waiting for an explanation.

It's all linked to Juan Antonio Pérez-Dominguez, or Fofo for short, who was the hero of my life until recently.

I think I should go back ten days and explain what happened.

As you know, during the time between the end of winter and the onset of summer, which this year was so short I barely had time to say the word "spring", Fofo fell in love and disappeared, and I'd heard nothing from him until last Tuesday.

That day, that ill-starred Tuesday at about five o'clock, when the shop was crowded with people, that is, Turks who chose to ignore any talk of a crisis and were still buying detective novels, I looked up and saw Fofo standing in the doorway.

You can guess how pleased I was.

Fofo had moved into Alfonso's house on Büyükada, the largest of the Prince's Islands. Apparently, he hadn't been to see me because he didn't come over to Istanbul very often. For those who don't know, I should explain that Büyükada is in the Marmara Sea, not the Mediterranean, and it takes a mere thirty minutes by sea bus to reach Istanbul. Actually, I would never board one of those claustrophobic things called sea buses even if it was only a ten-minute journey. I would rather sit on the deck of a ferry, sipping tea in the Marmara breeze.

Of course, having found Fofo, I wouldn't let him go. I called Selim immediately and asked him to make a reservation for that evening. We'd all have dinner together. Knowing that Selim loved to go to kebab restaurants in miserable areas of Istanbul like Eminönü, I made a point of saying I wanted to go to a proper restaurant.

Actually, it's not fair to use the word miserable to describe Eminönü, so I'll explain. Istanbul's most splendid open space is in Eminönü, but it's become victim to the Istanbul Municipality and Turkish city-planning, and now serves the nation as a central bus station. But that's another matter.

We'd arranged to meet Alfonso and Selim at eight o'clock at the Japanese restaurant in Elmadağ. I wanted to leave the shop early, go home, shower and change for dinner… I ask you, that was a very normal wish, wasn't it?

However, Fofo insisted that, instead of going home, I go across to the tea garden opposite the shop for a chat. He didn't just insist, he persisted until he got his way. He then proceeded to work himself up into such a rage that he ended up hurling insults at me. And what insults… If I had to go out to dinner in my work clothes, so what! Those middle-class ways of mine were pretty intolerable anyway. Didn't I realize there were more important things in life than my clothes, my sagging chin and my withering skin? At a time when the world was talking about the terrorist attack on the Twin Towers, when a serious war could break out at any moment, what did I spend my time worrying about? Did I have any idea how tedious I'd become? Was it no longer possible to have any sort of proper conversation with me?

As you've guessed, Fofo received an abrupt answer to that last question. There was no going out for dinner that night, and no introduction to Alfonso.

No, the sullen expression on my face had nothing to do with my row with Fofo. Nor the caterpillar that was eating away at my brain. I'd never force anyone into friendship; at my age I can't change, and I can't be bothered with people who are rude, vindictive or hateful.

My jumpiness had nothing to do with my approaching period, as Selim liked to claim at every opportunity. There's an international group of men, including my lover, who insist on the "menstrual theory" for anything relating to women that is irresolvable. Actually, I like men like this...

Anyway, to get back to this caterpillar business... Ever since I was a child, I've had a way of manipulating conversations in order to avoid subjects I don't like. I'm living proof that people don't change, aren't I?

So, for the last time. To get back to this caterpillar business...

The truth is I've had difficulty explaining the reason for the caterpillar.

... (short silence)

Maybe there are caterpillars like mine roaming around in the heads of some of you. If that's so, you understood me long ago. As for the rest of you... Don't bother trying to work it out. I won't waste your time; I'll just say what I have to say. The problem was this:

It had been accepted that Petra planned and carried out a perfect murder, yet she had never admitted it, and my uneasiness about it all was turning into a huge caterpillar that was gnawing away at my brain.

(A note to my dear reader: Those who don't like the caterpillar metaphor should email their suggestions for alternatives to katihirschel@web.de. Suggestions delivered personally at the shop will not be accepted.)

When I entered the shop the following morning, my face had the tired but determined expression of someone with a mission in life. I hadn't slept the previous night, or for several nights before that. I went straight to the phone and called Muazzez *Hanim*, who could put me in touch with Jean. Muazzez *Hanim* was Selim's secretary.

Five minutes later, Jean was on the other end of the line.

"Of course I remember you," he said, cutting short my self-introduction.

"I... I called you to ask you something... It might seem stupid to you, but..."

"Shall I be honest with you?"

Honest about what?

"Say it," I said.

"Nothing could seem so stupid to me as a woman like you being with Selim."

I coughed and cleared my throat.

"You remember we talked about the child murders at dinner that night... As far as I understand, you have information about all the children and their families."

"Hmmm."

"I was going to ask if you could fax me that information." I realized it was a strange request.

"I'm not going to ask why you're so interested in that case. It's up to you whether you tell me or not," he said in a serious voice.

"If there's no objection to you giving me the information I want, I'd rather not say," I said. I have to admit that, even after so many years, I would have found it difficult to construct that sentence in Turkish.

There was a moment's silence. I held my breath and waited.

"OK, I'll give you the file. But…" he said.

"Yes?"

"But it would take too long to fax. Our files are all kept on the computer. If you give me your email address, I'll send them to you."

I gave Jean the email address that I gave you, my dear readers. I didn't have to wait long. Ten minutes later, when I went online, a 183-page file was there in my inbox. The file contained police and court records, some of which were translated. Some were in French, some in German and others in languages I couldn't understand at all. It was up to me to wade through all that information to find what I was looking for.

However, I was prepared to do that.

I left the shop and customers to Pelin and set off home.

I read the German records, deciphered the French and tried to make something out of the Dutch, making notes as I went. By the time I'd finished the documents relating to the eighth child to be abducted and killed, it was already dark and much of the population was already asleep. What I was reading was heart-rending. I was hungry, my back ached from sitting at my desk all day, I'd split open a second packet of cigarettes and I hadn't managed to find a single piece of information that could save me from the caterpillar.

But somewhere there, in that 183-page file, there had to be what I was looking for.

I moved on to the ninth child.

The ninth child was from West Germany and was abducted from a refugee camp in Krefeld.

The child's date of birth… When abducted, the child wasn't even five. Not even five years old.

I shuddered. It was the youngest child so far. I pressed my hand to my forehead, thinking it was a miracle I hadn't developed a migraine yet. I lit another cigarette and continued reading.

Child's place of birth: Sofia.

Close relatives…

Mother.

Only the mother's name was there. The box for the father's name was empty.

Mother: Mitka Marinova.

The mother's application for asylum had been denied. One week before she was due to be sent back to her own country, her child was abducted.

Mother's address: k.k. Ilinden, bl.54 (vila7) et.3 1342 Sofia, Bulgaria.

Tel: (+359 2) 292 44 76.

I went out to the Bambi Büfe for a toasted cheese sandwich.

I awoke the next morning feeling a physical and psychological wreck. The details I'd learned had made me toss and turn all night. Even brushing my teeth didn't get rid of the bitter taste in my mouth. It was Saturday, but I was in no fit state to join Yılmaz or engage in cheerful gossip.

I called him up and said I couldn't come.

I went to the kitchen to make some coffee in order to muster up the courage to go back to the file that was waiting for me on the computer.

I was waiting for the water to boil for coffee, with my eyes fixed on the kettle, when suddenly it all clicked.

My thoughts went back to a June day three months earlier, when it was so hot that even the doves were perspiring. I was going up the steps of the villa in Yeniköy. As I went through the door, a coolness mixed with the damp smell of heavy antiques had greeted me. I'd passed through into the sitting room. But I'd wanted to sit on the veranda, not in that huge showcase of furniture. Before going out onto the veranda…

I wasn't alone.

The white-uniformed maid had been standing next to me, telling me how she'd learned Turkish. "I came from Bulgaria and started working here," she'd said.

"I came from Bulgaria," she'd said. From Bulgaria!

I went to my study to make a phone call. I couldn't help feeling that I was being stupid. My sensible readers would agree.

I dialled the number I'd noted down the previous evening.

There was a clicking sound. I waited. My heart was pounding. I continued to wait impatiently. The call didn't connect.

I pressed the redial button.

"The water for the coffee must have boiled away in the kitchen," I thought. Again, the number didn't connect.

That time I didn't press the redial button, I dialled the number. Should I have drunk my coffee and then called, I wondered.

I waited awhile and then, just as I was about to put the phone down, I finally heard the ringing tone. I'd got through! But if anyone picked up the telephone, what was I going to say and which language should I speak?

Someone did pick up the telephone. "Good morning," I said in English.

A reply in Bulgarian came from the other end.

"Do you speak English?" I asked in English. "Or German?" I quickly added.

A woman said something to me in Bulgarian again.

"Mitka Marinova," I said this time, instead of going through all the languages I knew.

The woman continued to say something in Bulgarian. "Mitka," I repeated loudly, as if our problem was not that we had no common language, but that we couldn't hear each other.

There was no reply. I looked around for my packet of cigarettes.

"Alo! You want Mitka, who are you?" said a male voice in German.

"I met Mitka in Germany. In Krefeld. I'm a friend," I said.

"Mitka isn't in Sofia. She's working in Turkey," he said.

I took a deep breath.

"Do you have a number where I can call her?" I asked. "We were good friends but I haven't heard from her for a long time. She may have mentioned me to you. My name's Tina. I'm from Ghana." Don't ask whether there are any women in Ghana called Tina, because I've no idea. And I'm sure the man on the telephone had no idea either.

"There is a number," he said. And he gave it to me.

I didn't call immediately. I allowed myself time to have a few coffees and cigarettes.

"Adana was good for you," I said.

He smiled and looked at his watch.

"We'll be late. Shall we go?" I said.

Selim left me outside the café in Yeniköy and went off to his office.

The moment I went through the battered door of the café, I saw the two women sitting at a table in the far corner. This time, the white-uniformed maid was wearing a yellow sweater. Her hair was tied back just as when I first saw her on that June day. She'd applied heavy rouge which was noticeable even from that distance.

As I made my way towards their table, I studied the woman sitting next to Mitka. She had a large nose, large lips and large eyes. Apart from her eyes, the most notable thing about her was her leopard-skin-print blouse. The way she was rubbing her hands up and down her arms suggested she knew the season for wearing sleeveless silk blouses was over…

I went and stood next to their table. It was clear that neither of them felt inclined to shake hands with me. "Hello," I said and sat down.

I was aware of them studying me as I took my cigarettes and lighter out of my bag. My nail varnish, the way I hung my handbag over the arm of the wooden chair, my hairstyle, the colour of my quickly applied eyeshadow…

"Have you had breakfast?" I asked.

They didn't reply.

"We haven't met," I said to the woman in the leopard-skin blouse.

"I know who you are," she said.

"But I don't know who you are," I said.

She raised her hand towards somebody and waved. A man standing near the door came running over to us.

"Yes, miss."

"Fetch me a sweater, Necmi. I'm cold."

"Right away," said Necmi.

I narrowed my eyes and looked at the woman.

"You're Yakut," I said.

Now I was excited.

"Why did you want to meet Mitka?" When she asked this question, her tone was so hostile that I felt I should object.

"No," I said, shaking my head. "Look, I'm not your enemy." I smiled at Mitka. "I just wanted to talk."

That was no good! This was no time to be pleasant, yet I'd just caved in straight away.

I asked the waiter to bring me a coffee.

"I know you spoke to Petra," said Yakut. "Petra was too much for you, and you thought Mitka would be a softer touch, yes? But there aren't just the two of you in this. You have me to reckon with as well, so act accordingly!" She banged the table with her dark, bony hand. The water bottle and glasses of Uludağ soda jolted, splashing their contents, which spread across the table and dripped onto the floor. Yakut pushed back her chair.

"You can't blackmail us!" she said through her teeth.

"I have no intention of blackmailing anyone."

"You'd better not!"

I looked around. The café was full of families with children and young people out to enjoy themselves.

"If you're relying on that idiot lawyer friend of yours…"

Was it hearing Selim referred to as an idiot that made me see red? Or was it that she seemed to think I needed someone to lean on?

I suddenly leaned forward, grabbed the collar of her leopard-skin blouse with my right hand and pulled her towards me. I held her chin in my hand, feeling the water that had just spilled onto the table creep up my arm.

"You're the idiot," I said, bringing her face right up to mine. "Watch it! Or I'll create a really bad scene here."

Letting go of her collar, I grasped her hair with my left hand. Mitka jumped to her feet and started shouting. I banged Yakut's face down onto the table, then let go of her hair as I heard the sound of feet running towards us. She sat back in her chair, holding her nose and looking as if she was about to faint, but it was her lip that was bleeding, not her nose.

"Miss!" said a man in a black suit. It wasn't Necmi. He had his eyes fixed on me, waiting for orders.

"It's nothing," said Yakut. "Go away." Then, as he made to go, she said, "Stop! Take Mitka home."

After they left, she covered her mouth with her hand, got up and went to the bathroom.

I lit a cigarette.

By the time Yakut returned, my coffee had arrived.

"How do I look?" she asked as she sat down.

I didn't reply.

"How do I look?" she repeated.

"Better than before," I said.

"They couldn't find me a sweater," she said, rubbing her arms with her hands to warm herself.

I was upset by the sight of this woman whose lip I had just burst open, and I wanted to give her my own sweater.

"Shall we go?" I asked. I didn't like being there any more. The other customers had stopped talking and were looking at us. I didn't blame them; I would have done the same.

"Let's sit here a bit longer," she said, clearly needing more time to collect herself.

"Shall I order some tea?" I asked.

"Coffee would be better, no sugar."

I beckoned to the waiter, who had been standing with his eyes fixed on us, and asked for two coffees with no sugar.

"You're a strange woman," said Yakut. Was that meant as a compliment?

"So are you," I said. "How did you get mixed up in this business?"

She fixed her eyes on some distant spot and seemed deep in thought. "Mmm. How did I get mixed up in this?" she murmured to herself.

No, actually that was not what I'd wanted to ask. I could have answered that question myself. Yakut was clearly a woman of principles and not afraid to extend a helping hand to anyone around her who was in need.

"Who did you know? Was it Mitka?" She looked at me vacantly. I needed to keep talking.

"I've no intention of going to the police," I said. "I'm curious, that's all. If you don't want to tell me, we'll forget about it."

She shrugged her shoulders.

"I know you've no intention of going to the police," she said. "Mitka works at my brother's house."

"I know," I said.

"You couldn't help noticing that she'd been through a dreadful experience."

And Mesut? Did he know too?

"Were Mesut and Yusuf aware that…" I was unable to finish my sentence.

"No, this was women's business," she said, adding with a smile: "A hair-dryer is very much a woman's weapon, don't you think?"

"Yes, a woman's weapon…" The waiter brought our coffees and I thanked him. "Who threw the hair-dryer into the bathtub?"

She pointed towards the cigarettes as if asking if she could take one. I picked up the packet.

"They're all wet."

She looked at the cigarettes and laughed.

"Who do you think threw the hair-dryer into the bath?"

"Petra," I said, without smiling.

She raised one eyebrow and nodded her head.

"Bravo."

"And you arranged everything."

"It was quite a job. It even involved persuading that lazy husband of mine to do some work. There were loads of actresses who would have been perfect for that part, so of course I had to work extra hard to make sure Petra got the part."

"OK. And Mitka?"

"She was crucial. If it hadn't been for her, I wouldn't even have known of Kurt Müller's existence."

"How did you find Petra? How did you know that her son was one of the victims?"

"There are excellent detectives who can find these things out."

"But no one even knew that Peter was Petra's child."

"My dear, take a good look at me. Do I look like a woman who would believe that tale about the sister in Korea?"

I looked at her huge eyes, her large nose and her thick lips.

"No," I said. "Definitely not." Looking at her huge eyes again, I said, "I'm far too hot. Let me give you my sweater."

"Are you sure we can't drop you off at home?" she asked, as the driver opened the door and she seated herself inside her luxury car.

"I'll get a taxi," I said.

"It's the first time anything like this has happened to me," she said, raising her hand to her lip. "And they say Germans are cowards."

"I went a bit too far."

"If you weren't so pretty, I might not have been able to forgive you," she said.

"Oh God," I said, "Let's not go into that. I've reached the age when I have to convince myself that beauty is of no importance."

"Oh, I'm not so sure about that," said Yakut.

Acknowledgements

I should say that while writing this, my first book and publication, I encountered various problems, and I would like to thank certain friends for their constant encouragement, support and constructive criticism. They include Rüstem Batum, Arzu Çağlan, Otto Diederichs, Tuğrul Eryılmaz, Neslihan Kurt, Fatih Özgüven, Canan Parlar and Yıldırım Türker.

I would also like to thank Professor of Forensic Medicine Hamit Hancı for giving me his time and for providing answers to my questions about certain unsavoury matters.